OPERATOR 5:
DEATH'S RAGGED ARMY

SECRET SERVICE OPERATOR #5™
AMERICA'S UNDERCOVER ACE

DEATH'S
RAGGED ARMY

By Curtis Steele

STEEGER BOOKS • 2021

PUBLISHING HISTORY

"Death's Ragged Army" originally appeared in the June/July, 1936 (Vol. 7, No. 2) issue of *Operator #5* magazine. Copyright © 2021 by Argosy Communications, Inc. All rights reserved.

CHAPTER 1
ARMY OF DOOMED

O N T H E twenty-second day of the invasion of the United States by the Purple Emperor, a crowd of stunned, hopeless men and women gathered in Union Square in New York City to hear a proclamation of the conqueror. The gray-shirted, steel-helmeted, stony-faced guards of the Central Empire used their sabers indiscriminately to keep the crowd in order. In the center of the square, a wide platform had been erected, and upon it was a gruesome block, with a groove in the top, upon which a man might rest his head before it was chopped from his body by the executioner.

A score of prisoners awaiting execution in a wooden cage on wheels near the platform drew the silent sympathy of the throng. But no voices were raised in protest, for the sabers of the guards were perilously close, and those guards were all too willing to plunge the shining blades into the throats of anyone who offered the slightest show of resistance.

It was nine o'clock in the morning, and the warm sun was bathing the city, its brightness offering sharp contrast to the destruction and havoc that lay everywhere. Though debris of the ten-day bombardment had all been cleared away by the forced labor of captive citizens, the crumbled walls of buildings all around the square, the gaping holes in the streets, testified to the extensive damage that had been done.

Suddenly, a stir ran through the sullen thousands in the square as a squat, broad-shouldered man stepped up on the platform in the center. He was naked from the waist up, and his chest was entirely covered with hair. His trousers were spattered with blood, and there were flecks of blood on his shoes. Black hair, matted and uncombed, fell over a low forehead to his eyes. He carried a huge broadsword on his shoulder, and when he

The Green Gas left countless thousands dead!

stopped beside the block, it took both hands to rest the cumbersome weapon on the floor.

A low growl arose from the throng at sight of him. Voices murmured: "The executioner! God, when will they stop?"

The executioner was keenly conscious of the hatred and revulsion he aroused, but rather than resenting it, he seemed to glory in it. His red tongue licked over his thick lips as his gaze rested gloatingly on the prisoners caged in the cell on wheels just below the platform. Nineteen of those prisoners were men; the twentieth was a girl. At first glance, it might have been difficult to distinguish her from the men; for she wore a man's trousers and an old slip-on sweater. But her bobbed chestnut hair could only belong to a woman; the soft curve of her white throat could never have belonged to a man.

She stood there in the cage, head thrown defiantly back, her clear blue eyes reflecting neither fear nor nervousness as she returned the executioner's insolent glance.

An elderly prisoner, who stood beside her, placed a hand on her shoulder. "Miss Elliot!" this man murmured. "I am old, and ready for death." He wore the uniform of a major of United States infantry, and his tunic was open, revealing a bloody bandage across his chest. "But for your sake I hope that this friend of yours, Operator 5, makes his boast to rescue you. You are too young and too beautiful to die!"

Diane Elliot shrugged, turned and gave the major a soft smile. "It's impossible, Major Fielding. See, they must have a thousand troops here. If Jimmy Christopher tried to save us, he would only be killed in the attempt. And he's needed—badly needed. He—"
SHE STOPPED speaking as a drum began to roll sonorously, and a double file of soldiers in gray began to push away through the throng toward the platform. They were escorting an officer of the Central Empire, whose gray uniform was decorated with red, braided tassels, whose chest bore a dozen medals, and whose black armband carried the reproduction

4

of the crossed broadswords and
the severed head, the insignia of
the Central Empire. It was under
that banner that the goose-stepping troops of the Purple Emperor
had conquered Europe and crossed
the Atlantic to invade the United
States.

This officer mounted the steps
to the platform, and a sudden hush fell upon the crowd in the
square as the drums ceased to roll. He was tall, slim, arrogant,
with a small, waxed moustache and cold eyes which seemed to
view the prisoners as so many sheep to be slaughtered.

He stepped to the microphone which had been set up just
in front of the execution block, and unrolled a sheet of paper,
He read from this in a deep, guttural voice which was carried to
every corner of the square by amplifiers:

"In the name of the august Maximilian, Lord of the Central
Empire, Master of Europe and Asia, be it known: That the
armies of the Central Empire are everywhere victorious. The
American troops have been flung back, westward to Lake Erie,
and southward to the Susquehanna River. Your President has
fled from your Capital. Your troops are demoralized. They cannot
stand against our modern weapons and our veteran troops. The
Emperor has sworn that within three weeks more, your entire
country shall bend its knee and swear allegiance to him, just as
all the nations of the eastern hemisphere have already done; and
just as Canada has already done. Within two months, he shall

be the master of the Americas—the Emperor of the greatest empire ever seen upon this earth. Like Alexander, he shall seek new worlds to conquer. His power and his might shall be felt wherever men have knees to bend, and lips to kiss the ground!"

Diane Elliot, listening with flushed face, turned and said scornfully to Major Fielding: "What a conceited ass that Maximilian must be!"

She said it loud enough so that, in the pause between the words of the officer, that dignitary heard her plainly. He frowned at her, but his frown changed almost at once to a taunting smile of mockery. He went on:

"Those who do not bend the knee in token of allegiance to our Emperor shall bend it to the executioner's block. Today, twenty who have refused to take the oath shall lose their heads. Among them is a woman. Diane Elliot! Step up!"

At a motion of the officer's hand, two guards swung open the door of the cage, grinned nastily at the girl. She bore herself coolly, holding her slender body erect. One by one, she shook hands with the other prisoners. Major Fielding held her hand tight, and there were two drops of moisture in his eyes.

"You are very brave, Miss Elliot. If only Operator 5 could—"

She shook her head slightly. "I'm afraid it's too late, Major. Jimmy Christopher can't perform miracles. I—good-by, Major!" She closed her eyes for a moment, opened them swiftly, then tore her hand from the elderly officer's and turned, walked resolutely out through the door of the cage, down the four short steps to the ground. The two soldiers seized her roughly, twisted her hands behind her, and tied them. Then they pushed her up on to the platform. She stood there, with the eyes of thousands of men and women upon her; men and women who secretly envied her courage in refusing to take the oath of fealty to the conqueror, and who almost wished that they themselves were brave enough to step up there and die with her.

The officer in gray bowed to her ironically. "Madame," he said, smiling thinly, "the Emperor, in his august clemency, has ordered me to grant you one last chance. If you will take the oath now, your life will be spared!"

A DEEP sigh went up from the packed thousands who were craning their necks toward the platform of death. Diane could almost feel the silent entreaties of all those people. Behind her, she heard the hoarse, tortured voice of Major Fielding: "Do it, Miss Elliot. For God's sake, take the oath!"

Diane smiled a little, wanly. She squared her shoulders, and her little chin came up an inch. Her clear, blue eyes met those of the gray-uniformed officer. She said: "No! Thank your Emperor for me, and tell him that I would rather be dead than his subject!"

The officer's lip curled scornfully. "You are a fool, Miss Elliot!" He stepped closer to her, spoke so that only she could hear. "You are being given this chance because the Emperor does not want you to become a national heroine. You are foolish not to accept. What is a little oath? When your head is cut off, you will be dead a long time. You are young and beautiful, and you have much to live for. If you will take the oath, I will see that you are given a safe conduct through the lines. You may rejoin your countrymen. I, Colonel Mainz, promise this to you!"

Diane shook her head. "No! You've executed thousands of

Americans in the last two weeks, Colonel Mainz. But I shall be the first woman. Perhaps that will be the spark that will spur our men on to hurl your armies back. That's what you're afraid of, Colonel, isn't it?" she taunted, as she saw him bite his lip in vexation. "You have huge guns that outrange our biggest ordnance. You have horrid chemicals that wipe out whole towns and whole regiments. But you are afraid that they wouldn't avail if the spirit of 1776 were once more awakened in Americans. And my execution may do it!"

Colonel Mainz glared at her. "The Emperor is not afraid. We have already proved in Europe and in Asia that we are irresistible. Here, too, we have conquered eight states at a cost of less than five hundred troops. But the Emperor wishes this conquest to be as swift as possible. He does not want your countrymen to exhaust the resources of the nation in hopeless defense. That is why he will grant you life if you will take the oath—"

"I'm sorry, Colonel," Diane said firmly. "I insist on being executed!"

Colonel Mainz stepped back angrily. "So be it!" He motioned to the two soldiers, and they seized her once more, forced her over toward the block. The executioner, who had been watching her avidly, licked his lips, and raised his huge broadsword. Diane knelt, and one of the soldiers callously ripped away the neck of her sweater, exposing her white, soft throat. Then he placed a hand on her head, forced it down upon the block.

A gasp of dismay arose from the throng. Down in the cage, Major Fielding and the other prisoners watched with hot eyes and gritted teeth. The major exclaimed: "God! Where's that

Operator 5? He smuggled a note into prison yesterday. It promised that he wouldn't let her die. And here she is on the block! *God—!*"

The executioner took his stance alongside the block, the huge broadsword poised above his head, gripped in his two hairy hands....

A MILE from Union Square, upon the terrace outside an office of the Empire State Building, stood a bevy of officers. They all wore uniforms lavishly decorated with medals and gold braid. Their armbands all bore the insignia of the crossed broadswords and the severed head. And they all fawned in servile adulation upon the short, squat man with the sharp nose and the eagle eyes who was looking through a pair of binocular telescopes toward the scene on Union Square. This man wore an ermine cape over his officer's uniform. His hands were pudgy. Upon the little finger of his left hand was a seal ring. The engraving on that seal was the same as the insignia on the armbands of the officers—the crossed broadswords and the severed head. He bore a remarkable resemblance to Napoleon Bonaparte. He was the Emperor Maximilian I, Lord of the Central Empire, Master of Europe and Asia, and in a fair way to becoming the Master of America also.

He put down his telescope, turned to his officers. "Well," he said in a guttural language of Central Europe, "it seems that the girl wishes to die." His lips twisted in a half smile. "In a few minutes the sword will be raised to fall upon her pretty neck. Oscar—" he addressed one of his officers, the most gaudily decorated of them all—"you are sure that this guerilla, Operator 5, is going to try to rescue her?"

The officer bowed low, servilely. "He will surely attempt it, Imperial Highness. I read the note which he smuggled into the prison. It said that she was to have courage, that he had a plan to save her. And from what we know of him, Highness, he will not fail to appear!"

Maximilian smiled slowly. "You have made all arrangements?"

"Everything is in readiness, Highness. Men are posted in every building around Union Square. Every street leading away from there is covered. Fifty machine guns are planted in windows commanding the square. Two hundred of our picked men are scattered through the crowd around the platform. Once this Operator 5 appears, it is a certainty that he will never leave there alive. The trap is baited well, Highness, and I have changed the date of the execution from this afternoon to now, as you know. He will have to rush his plans before they are complete, and he will surely fall into the trap. We will be rid of this guerrilla, once and for all!"

The Emperor nodded. "That is good, Oscar. This Operator 5 has done much damage. He polluted the drinking water; he blew up an ammunition train, he spiked our long-range gun with which we were to shell Washington. His guerrilla band has slowed up our scheduled advance. By now we should have driven these Americans back to the Mississippi. He must die!"

Oscar bowed, rubbed his hands. "He shall die, Highness—within a very few minutes!"

Maximilian picked up the binoculars again. "Well, let us

watch what happens. I shall enjoy this. It was clever of you, Oscar, to use this woman whom he loves as bait. And it was clever of you to have paved the way for him to smuggle in the note. I am pleased with you." He raised the glass to his eyes, focused it once more on Union Square....

CHAPTER 2
REIGN OF TERROR

A T EIGHT o'clock that morning, an hour before the scheduled executions in Union Square, a young man and a boy might have been seen on the steps of the New York Public Library, inconspicuous among a crowd of dejected citizens who were reading various notices posted here and in other public places throughout the city.

Gray-uniformed, hard-faced soldiers stood on guard everywhere. Details of troops patrolled the streets, stopping citizens, questioning and searching them, and often taking them away for further questioning. At sight of such arrests, men shivered. For they knew that those people would never be seen or heard from again until they knelt some morning to rest their necks upon the executioner's chopping block.

The crowd around the notices was strangely quiet, dispirited. The young man and the boy did not speak to each other, but worked their way in close to the big doors on the Fifth Avenue side, where the notices were posted. There were two that seemed to interest them particularly. They were printed in English. The first one read as follows:

PROCLAMATION!

Maximilian I, by the grace of God, Emperor of Europe and Asia, now asserts his supreme sovereignty over the continent of North America! All those residing in conquered territory must obey the following rules:

1. Each man, woman and child must register with the commandant in charge of his local area. He will receive an identification card. Anyone found in the streets without such card shall be immediately sentenced to decapitation without further trial.

2. No person shall carry arms of any description. Discovery of any weapons upon any person shall be punishable by instant death.

3. All persons over the age of fourteen shall perform two hours of labor daily at the command of the commander of the military forces. Times to report for such labor will be assigned when identification cards are issued.

4. All stores of food in homes or business places shall be forthwith turned over to the commandant of the area. Food will then be rationed out at the discretion of the commandant. All persons in whose homes food of any description is discovered shall be immediately executed REGARDLESS OF AGE OR SEX.

5. Every person must take an oath of allegiance to Maximilian I, and swear to be his faithful subject. When the oath has been taken, identification cards will be marked....

There was more, but the young man and the boy did not wait

to read the rest. They glanced at each other, and there was a bitterness in their faces as their eyes met. The young man nudged the boy, and they moved over to the second notice, posted on the other side of the doors. There was an equally large crowd here, and they were avidly reading its contents under the watchful eyes of the armed guards.

TAKE NOTICE!

Anyone having knowledge of the whereabouts of the guerrilla known as Operator 5 is ordered to report same at once to the commandant of the area. Any person who shall furnish information leading to the capture or death of the person known as Operator 5 shall be rewarded by exemption from all labor requirements for himself and his family; he shall be supplied with adequate rations, and if he so desires, shall be given a post with the provisional government.

But any person who shall be found to have given aid or comfort to the said Operator 5 shall be decapitated without delay, together with all his family. By order of His Imperial Highness, Maximilian I, Emperor of Europe and Asia.

Signed,

Baron Oscar zu Lambrecht,

General, Commanding Occupied Territory of New York.

The boy and the young man read through the notice carefully. Then they glanced at each other, and the lips of the young man quirked into a wry smile. "Looks bad for this Operator 5, Tim," he said. Though he was dressed in a pair of greasy, gray trousers

13

and a dirty khaki shirt, this young man seemed to have a degree of poise and assurance that contrasted oddly with the dejected attitude of the others in the crowd.

The boy, too, seemed to be strangely different. Freckle-faced, with an impertinently tilted Irish nose and an infectious smile, he did not appear on the surface to be very deeply affected by the catastrophe that had befallen his country.

A casual observer might have ascribed this lack of feeling to the lad's evident youth—he was only in his middle teens— but a glimpse into the boy's earnest, serious eyes would have convinced such an observer that this attitude of unconcern was only a pose. He looked up now at his older companion. "Spiking that Big Bertha of theirs yesterday was the last straw, Jimmy. Maximilian will never rest now, till he has your head in the basket."

Jimmy Christopher—Operator 5 of the United States Intelligence—nodded somberly. "I'm afraid, Tim," he said very low. "Afraid for our country. We've let them push us back to the Great Lakes. Our guns are child's toys compared to their high-powered weapons. Our countrymen have lived softly, in comfort, for

Jimmy Christopher

too long. We're way behind in preparedness. There's nothing to stop Maximilian from mastering the continent!"

The boy, Tim, looked up with a curious sort of confidence at Jimmy Christopher. "You can do it, Jimmy!" he breathed softly. "You've done it before. They—"

He stopped as a burly man alongside of them, reading the reward notice, growled: "Damn it, look at that! Do they think any one would be low enough to betray Operator 5?" He laughed harshly. "I wish to God I could help Operator 5 to strike a blow for liberty!"

Jimmy Christopher turned, and scanned the man's face sharply. He started as he recognized the man's face. "You're Plugger Dugan—the heavyweight champion—aren't you?" he asked.

The man nodded. He glanced appraisingly at Jimmy Christopher and the boy, Tim. He was five feet eleven and a half inches tall, and his shoulder muscles bulged under his coat. He had three gold teeth in the front of his upper row, and his nose was twisted, battered—tokens of the hundred ring battles that he had fought and won before reaching the championship. Jimmy Christopher had seen Plugger Dugan win the championship fight. Dugan was perhaps the greatest boxer of all time, for in addition to being supremely skillful with his hands and feet, he had the ruggedness and the courage to be able to "take it." And the marks on his face were the signs of that ability. He had "taken" plenty in his ring career, but he boasted that he had never been off his feet in the ring.

"That's me," he said in answer to Jimmy Christopher's question. "Plugger Dugan. The fighter. The guy they paid a million bucks to see in Madison Square Garden." He laughed bitterly. "An' here I am, not raisin' a finger to fight for my country. I'd give my right hand," he added fiercely, "to be able to join up with Operator 5's band!"

Jimmy Christopher glanced around cautiously. Though the crowd was thick, no one was paying attention to them. Men and women were whispering in groups, furtively, under the eyes of the guards. No one had heard their short conversation.

Jimmy moved a little closer to Plugger Dugan. "Maybe," he said slowly, "you could have your wish—without giving your right hand!"

Dugan's mouth fell open. He stared queerly at Jimmy. "What do you mean by that crack?" he demanded.

Operator 5 smiled. "When we leave here, you follow us, Plugger. Stay about fifty feet behind. We'll take you to—where you want to go!"

"You mean—you'll take me to Operator 5?"

"Perhaps."

The attention of the crowd was attracted by a gray-uniformed petty officer who pushed through roughly, and tacked another notice on the doors. Jimmy Christopher's eyes darkened as he read:

TAKE NOTICE!

The execution of the twenty persons scheduled for two o'clock this afternoon will take place at nine-thirty this morning instead. By order of His Imperial Majesty, Maximilian I.

Signed,

17

Baron Oscar zu Lambrecht,
General, Commanding Occupied Territory of New York.

The freckle-faced boy clutched Operator 5's sleeve with sudden urgency. "Jimmy! That means Diane will be killed this morning! We've got to change our plans!"

Jimmy Christopher's hands were clenched tightly at his sides. The muscles of his jaws bulged as he clamped them tight together. For a moment he thought swiftly, then turned, snapped to Plugger Dugan: "Follow us!"

With Tim at his side, and the big prizefighter puzzledly trailing them, Operator 5 made his way around the corner, and walked swiftly west on Forty-second Street....

THE STREETS were a shambles. The concrete was broken up, and vast holes yawned, from which water seeped, changing Forty-second Street into a river. Men walked ankle-deep in water. The bombardment had been particularly terrific here, and all the buildings on the north side were demolished, their walls lying crumbled in the seepage from the water mains and sewage system. There was no transportation, no telephone service, and no electric light in New York. Field telephones, of course, had been set up by the Central Empire army, but aside from that, New York might have been an early nineteenth-century town. The Public Library, the Empire State Building and a few others were the only structures which still remained more or less intact, and these were being utilized by the invaders for military and governmental purposes.

The same havoc had been wrought in a hundred other American cities in New England, New York and Pennsylvania.

When Maximilian Steig, the Dictator of Balkaria, had declared himself Emperor, America entertained no suspicion that within less than a year he would reduce our greatest cities to a mass of ruins. Not even when his superbly militarized nation made war on the rest of Europe, conquered it nation by nation, did we feel any sense of danger. But when Maximilian finally did what Napoleon  had failed to accomplish—namely, to consolidate all of Europe and parts of Asia under a vicious empire of which he was the absolute lord and master—we still did not comprehend his ultimate purpose.

Then Maximilian took a step that even Napoleon would never have dared. Napoleon was not a brilliant naval commander, in spite of his ability on land. Maximilian, however, now controlled the greatest military and naval geniuses of Europe, but also all the continental manpower and the ships. His navy, when he set sail for the conquest of Canada, was the greatest that had ever been assembled by a single ruler. It combined the navies of the nations he had conquered. It carried guns and chemicals for warfare which were the products of the most highly-developed armament factories of the world. It was too late for the United States to begin to compete in an armament race.

We had thought that our security was assured by the three thousand miles of ocean between us and the troops of Maximilian. Those three thousand miles became nothing. It took three weeks and two days for the huge armada to make the crossing. Canada offered but feeble resistance; the mother country had already succumbed to the warlord. We flung hastily recruited troops to the aid of our neighbor, but they could not stand against the highly-militarized, perfectly-functioning war machine of Maximilian. Canada fell. And the brutal invasion of the United States began.

Our munitions factories began to run full blast. Our airplane plants struggled frantically to turn out flying machines. But Maximilian had them already. He didn't have to wait. Our defenses were swept away, crumbled before the goose-stepping troops of the invader. We were swept out of New England in twenty-two days. The reign of terror began....

TWO WEEKS before, Jimmy Christopher and freckle-faced Tim Donovan had worked their way through the enemy lines, and Jimmy had recruited a small force of men who carried on guerrilla warfare, trying as well to build up an organization within the occupied territory that might be used some day for turning upon the invader. For it was admitted by the United States General Staff that there was no possibility of halting Maximilian. He might be slowed up by the feeble resistance which we could offer, but he would eventually subjugate the entire land. More and more troops were now pouring across from Europe. Our own big guns, which had performed so impressively in war maneuvers, proved to be outmoded by the secret development of Maximilian's war scientists. Our own scientists had been discouraged from such investigations in the past, for the pacifists in our government had invariably contended against large appropriations for the development of war inventions; whereas in Europe each new invention was seized upon avidly.

THE NEW gas, which had practically destroyed every living soul in the state of Maine before the invasion was even begun, was an example of this. Maximilian had not used that gas in Europe. He had used it in Canada, and we had not believed the reports. But the truth of those reports was brought home to us with all-too-terrible results when Maine was swept of life in six hours. Such a gas had been written of in fiction, but had never been conceived as a practical possibility. Maximilian had used it sparingly so far; not at all since the Maine catastrophe. He could accomplish his objective without it. But the United States General Staff was daily in fear that it would be used again, and in consequence dared not concentrate a very large body of troops in any one area.

It was conceded by the General Staff that Maximilian could wipe out the entire population of the United States in two weeks by the use of his *Green Gas,* as it was commonly known. But it was also recognized that a vast land with a hundred million corpses in it would be of little value to the conqueror. So it was easy to understand the Emperor's decision against promiscuous use of the *Green Gas.*

Nevertheless, the conquest went on unchecked. The country which had once turned the tide of victory against Germany in the first World War now found itself rapidly being reduced to vassalage because of its lack of preparation.

"Let others beware the same fate!

Executioner, do your duty!"

DEATH'S RAGGED ARMY

Jimmy Christopher had attempted tirelessly, from the first day of the invasion, to find some clue to the nature of the *Green Gas*. He had covered his activities under the cloak of guerrilla warfare within the enemy lines. But he was no nearer success in that direction today than he had been twenty days ago. And it seemed now that his hand was being forced by the approaching execution of Diane Elliot.

As he made his way across Forty-second Street, with Tim Donovan beside him, and Plugger Dugan trailing behind, gangs of men were working under the supervision of armed guards, clearing away the debris. These men were former businessmen, clerks, storekeepers. Everyone in the city had to perform his tithe of labor for the invaders, and they were being put to work clearing the streets. They worked in two feet of water, laboring with heavy slabs of masonry from the fallen buildings, carrying them to wheelbarrows, then laboriously wheeling the barrows across town to the East River, where the debris was loaded on barges and carried away to be dumped.

The three threaded their way among arrogant Central Empire officers, among dejected citizens who kept their eyes on the ground lest they give offense to their new masters.

All the way across town Jimmy led the way, then under the Express Highway to a spot along the riverfront where two bicycles were cached under a tarpaulin. He removed the tarpaulin, waited for Dugan to come up with them. The prizefighter exclaimed: "Say! Where'd you get them?"

Jimmy grinned. "Those are what we use for transportation. Can you ride a bicycle?"

"Can I ride one? Why, I train on one!"

"Okay," Jimmy said crisply. "Follow me along the riverfront. Tim, you'll have to ride on my handlebars."

"Hey, wait a minute!" Dugan said. "Who are you, anyway? An' where are we goin'?"

Jimmy Christopher faced him, said quietly: "You wanted to meet Operator 5, didn't you?"

"Right."

"I am Operator 5."

Dugan's eyes widened. "You! Why, you're too young—!"

"Not much younger than you—and you're the world's heavyweight boxing champion."

Dugan smiled. "Believe me, I'd rather be Operator 5. Why, man, let me shake your hand. You've put the fear o' God into this here Maximilian. I'm with you—to the limit!"

THEY SHOOK, and Jimmy's hand met the fighter's in a hard grip, while their eyes pledged mutual loyalty. Jimmy introduced Tim. "This is Tim Donovan. Don't let his freckles deceive you. He's a bright kid. He's been my assistant for a couple of years. He's too young to be admitted to the Intelligence, but when he grows up he'll be a wow. He's a little fresh, but don't mind him—it's just his youthful spirits."

Tim glowered at Jimmy, and gripped the hand that Plugger smilingly extended to him.

Jimmy Christopher began to explain to Dugan: "Tim and I are going to attempt something that may mean our death. I'm going to take you part of the way downtown, and then send you

25

to headquarters. If we don't show up within a few hours, there will be others there in our guerrilla band to take charge—"

"Hey!" Dugan shouted. "Hold everything. Could I ask maybe what you're planning to do that's so dangerous?"

Jimmy Christopher hesitated, then shrugged. "You may as well know, so that if we don't show up, you can tell the boys what's happened to us. "We're going to attempt to rescue a young lady who is to be executed in about one hour. We're going to make a stab at snatching her right off the execution block."

"That's good," said Dugan. "Let's go. How we gonna pull it?"

Jimmy shook his head. "I have no right to involve anybody else in this. It's a personal matter with Tim and myself. The young lady in question is very dear to us—"

Dugan broke in. "It's Miss Elliot, isn't it? The girl reporter for the Amalgamated Press? The one who won't take the oath of allegiance to the Purple Emperor?"

"That's right. How do you know?"

Dugan laughed. "Maybe there's no newspapers, but there's a grapevine. Everybody knows about her. They say if she's killed it'll be the greatest mistake Maximilian ever made. It'll arouse the people. She's the one that wrote that article attacking Maximilian the day he marched into New York. Everybody thinks she's great—the guts she needed to write that! Come on, boys, this is gonna be the darbs—"

"Wait," said Jimmy. "I've got to tell you—the chances of getting away with what we've planned are about one in four million. If you come with us, you may be lying in Union Square in an hour from now, riddled by machine-gun bullets; or you may be marching up to the block to have your head chopped off."

Dugan waved him aside. "To hell with that. I want a chance to do something. This is it. Try an' keep me from it."

Suddenly Jimmy Christopher smiled. "I think we'll get along fine together, Plugger," he said softly.

"That's what I think!" Tim Donovan chimed in.

CHAPTER 3
OPERATOR 5'S SKIRMISHERS

AS DIANE ELLIOT rested her head upon the executioner's block, a thousand thoughts raced through her mind in the moment's interval before the gleaming broadsword was to descend. Jimmy Christopher had written that he would not let her die. Jimmy had never made a promise that he had not kept. She knew that he would move heaven and earth to rescue her, that he would even make a hopeless attempt rather than let her perish in this way. There was only one explanation of his failure to appear—he must be dead. Almost with fierce joy she awaited the deadly *swish* which she knew would accompany the blow of the broadsword.

Long ago she had told Jimmy Christopher that she did not want to live longer than he. As Operator 5, he had consecrated his life to the service of his country. Danger and the constant threat of death rode ever at his elbow. And Diane, as the star reporter of the Amalgamated Press, had her own career. But this did not quench the mutual affection that had sprung up

27

between them. It might be that the peaceful comfort and the quiet of settled married life might never be for these two, to whom danger was the very essence of life. But Diane felt that if there were no longer a Jimmy Christopher in the world, who let her occasionally share his perils and his adventures, she would prefer not to be alive. Now she was having an adventure of her own; and Jimmy was not here to share it.

She heard Colonel Mainz's cold voice intone: "Diane Elliot! By order of His Imperial Majesty, Maximilian I, Emperor of Europe and Asia, the sentence of death is about to be executed upon you. Let others beware lest the same fate be theirs. Executioner! Do your duty!"

Diane's spine tingled as she awaited the fall of the sword which she could not see. She was unable to move her head, for her hair was in the grip of one of her guards, who stood on the other side of the block. She was strangely cool, almost detached about the whole thing. When was that blow going to be struck? She wondered if she would be conscious for that instant after her head was severed, and while it was rolling on the bloody platform. She remembered that people who had been guillotined during the French revolution had been known to blink their eyes, even though their heads were no longer part of their bodies. It would be an experience to feel one's self beheaded. Suppose her head lived on? Absurd. Suddenly she laughed aloud. She caught her breath. Was she becoming hysterical? This was no way to die. God! *Why didn't he strike?*

Abruptly, she became conscious of loud, explosive noises in the near distance. There were shouts all about from the throng in the square, and she suddenly felt her guard's grip on her hair become relaxed. She raised her head, remaining upon her knees. The executioner had stepped back from the block, and had lowered his ponderous sword. All eyes were fixed toward the west, from which direction there came a constant series of staccato, sharp explosions like the firing of sub-machine guns. Colonel Mainz was peering in that direction, frowning.

The guard who had been holding Diane's hair forgot about her in his excitement. He stepped to the edge of the platform, elbowing the executioner out of the way so he could get a better view of the street over the heads of the crowd. The distant firing increased in intensity.

And suddenly a glad light came into Diane's eyes. From out of the wreckage of buildings at the corner of Fourteenth Street and the square, a familiar figure came running. She recognized at once the lithe young body of Tim Donovan. He ran directly toward the platform, shouting: "They're attacking from the river! The Americans are attacking!"

COLONEL MAINZ swore luridly. He motioned to the drummer just below the platform. "Sound the formation call!" he ordered. At once the drum rolled its summons, and gray-uniformed soldiers from all over the square pushed through the crowd to its edge, fell into formation. Out from the side streets came more soldiers. It was a tribute to the thoroughgoing efficiency of the Central Empire troops that it took them less than four minutes to fall in from the time the drum began to sound.

In one minute more, they were marching toward the river. Colonel Mainz spoke rapidly to the executioner: "Remain here,

Willfred. Guard the prisoners. If this is a counterattack by those fools of Americans, we will dispose of them shortly."

He leaped from the platform, ran to take command of the column of troops. The alarm had spread to the rest of the city, and bugles were blowing in various other sections as troops hurried toward the river in answer to the alarm. The firing had ceased, and there was an ominous silence.

Diane had kept her eyes on the figure of Tim Donovan. After giving the first alarm, he had made himself as inconspicuous as possible, and Mainz, with the troops at his back, passed right by him without giving a thought to the apparent incongruity of an American boy warning them of an attack by Americans.

The great mob of men and women in the square remained quiet, cowed by the half-dozen machine-gun crews stationed at the corners of Union Square.

The executioner, Willfred, turned and gazed sourly at Diane. His small eyes glared at her, like a beast of prey that has been cheated of its game. Diane glanced down at Major Fielding and the other condemned prisoners in the cage on wheels, and threw the major a brave little smile. The driver of the team of horses which were hitched to the wagon had leaped off his seat and run around to the other side of the platform so as to be able to see the action. But the guard at the door of the cage still stood there alertly, with his rifle ready. There was no chance to rush him, and even if that were possible, there were still the machine guns at the fringes of the crowd to be considered. Escape was still hopeless in spite of the timely diversion.

And then, suddenly, hope sprang in the breast of Diane

Elliot. There appeared, pushing his way through the crowd in spite of their sullen looks, a young Central Empire officer, in the full uniform of a staff colonel. He had his revolver out, and shouted arrogantly to people in the crowd: "Out of my way, swine! Make way for the Emperor's messenger!"

Resentfully, way was made for him, until he stood at the foot of the platform. He glanced up, and his eyes met those of Diane Elliot. She had a hand at her throat, and there was a strange light of excited happiness in her face. For the young man in the uniform of the Central Empire staff officer was one whom she knew very well indeed, and from whom she had nothing to fear. He was Jimmy Christopher!

The troops under Colonel Mainz had already left the square, and the firing near the river seemed to redouble in intensity. Shouts began to arise from the crowd. A little of the old spirit of Americanism began to be evident once more.

"Hooray for the Yanks! Give it to 'em, boys! If we only had guns!"

But the shouts ceased abruptly as the machine-gun crew at the south end of the square fired a short burst over their heads. They realized that they would all be mowed down mercilessly at the first overt act on their part.

JIMMY CHRISTOPHER, in his strange uniform, called up to the executioner, speaking the tongue of the Central Empire with an enviable fluency; "You! Executioner! Bring that woman down! The Emperor wishes her and the other prisoners to be removed to a place of safety! The execution is to be postponed!"

The executioner bowed, his eyes on the imposing uniform. "Yes, Excellency! At once!"

He seized Diane's arm, led her down the steps, and over to the cage. As she passed Jimmy, she threw him a quick glance, but he did not show by so much as the flicker of an eyelid that he knew her or was interested in her personally. She allowed herself to be pushed roughly up into the tumbril, and Major Fielding eagerly clasped her hands.

"Miss Elliot!" the major exclaimed. "It's a miracle! Why, the sword was about to fall when the firing began. Your friend, Operator 5, must be at the back of this!"

Diane smiled queerly. "You don't know the half of it, Major!"

She was shaking a little, and her hands were cold. The ordeal she had just gone through was no light one. The average girl would either have fainted or become hysterical by this time, after having been so near a gruesome death. Diane had to grit her teeth to keep herself to giving way to the weak dizziness which suddenly assailed her. The reaction of being suddenly snatched from the jaws of destruction was a terrific one.

She felt the major's paternal arm about her shoulders, and straightened. Dimly, she was aware that Jimmy Christopher and the executioner had both climbed up into the driver's seat of the tumbril, heard the executioner say:

"Where shall we take the prisoners, Excellency?" And she heard Jimmy, still talking in the man's native tongue, which she understood fairly well: "Drive away from the square, quickly. Drive north!"

The tumbril got under way, while the two uniformed guards cleared a path for it through the crowd. Once past the edge of the throng, the horses began to trot, keeping to the extreme sides of the streets in order to avoid the ruts and shell holes. Looking back, Diane saw Tim Donovan come trotting after them. He was waving, and Diane waved back to him.

Major Fielding frowned, said: "Who's that boy, Miss Elliot? And where do you think they're taking us? I don't think your Operator 5 will have done you much good. That counterattack will surely be repulsed, and the execution will only have been delayed a few hours. They were quick to get us away from there—"

Diane laughed suddenly, a clear, tinkling laugh. Major Fielding stared at her, thinking that the strain had been too much for her. The executioner turned around in the driver's seat also, and grimaced. He said in broken English: "Do not laugh, pretty one." He patted the sword which lay at his side on the driver's seat, between himself and Jimmy Christopher.

"My blade will taste your blood—fear not. We will put you in the jail for safety—"

"No, my friend," Jimmy Christopher interrupted. "We're not going to the jail!" He was poking a revolver into the man's side. "You will turn off quickly, and drive east, where I shall tell you to go. If we meet a patrol on the way, you will say nothing to them—unless you prefer to die very quickly!"

The executioner gasped. "But, Excellency—"

Tim Donovan

"I'm not an Excellency!" Jimmy snapped. "I'm Operator 5!"

Willfred's eyes opened wide in horror. "Operator 5! But no! That uniform—"

Jimmy laughed mirthlessly. "One of your officers was indiscreet enough to wander alone in a dark street last night. I—er—induced him to lend me his uniform. Now"—his voice crackled—"turn right. And slow up a little, so that boy can catch up with us."

Willfred obeyed. In a moment, Tim Donovan had swung up, clinging to the rail at the side of the driver's seat. He grinned. "Hello, Di! I bet you thought we flopped on you!"

The prisoners in the cage had all pushed up toward the front, firing questions at Jimmy. "But that shooting—" demanded Major Fielding—"what is all that? Let us go to the aid of those boys who are attacking. At least we can die fighting—"

JIMMY INTERRUPTED him, laughing. "That isn't shooting, Major. We looted a firecracker storehouse down on Vesey Street yesterday. We linked the big crackers up, and a gentleman named Dugan set them off. When they explode one after the other like that, they sound just like machine-gun fire. When Colonel Mainz and his goose-steppers get there, they'll find nothing at all. Dugan's going to meet us at headquarters. And all you gentlemen are invited to become members of Operator 5's Partisan Skirmishers. We'll keep Willfred, here, for a mascot!"

The tumbril had turned east at Twenty-third Street, and

at First Avenue Jimmy made Willfred go north again. To the eager questions of Diane and the other prisoners, he explained that he and his small band of guerrillas had made their head-quarters in the ruins of Bellevue Hospital, which had been demolished by shellfire during the bombardment except for the powerhouse, over at the edge of the East River. They had two powerboats moored at the landing there, and were thus enabled to make night forays and to disappear quickly after a raid. So far they had successfully hidden their base of operations from the searchers of the Emperor Maximilian. But the retreat was a dangerous one, because as the city was being cleaned up, the Central Empire troops were coming closer and closer to discovering the powerhouse and its strange tenants. Working with some of the machinery that they had found there, Jimmy Christopher and his men had rigged up a radio, with which they maintained communication with the American forces, and had so far succeeded in relaying valuable information to the General Staff—information which had been picked up by patriotic men and women in the city who risked immediate execution by working as spies and observers right under the nose of the invaders.

The tumbril passed several enemy patrols on the way up First Avenue, but Jimmy's firm pressure of the gun in Willfred's side kept the surly, glowering executioner from giving the fatal alarm. Major Fielding was eagerly pumping questions at Jimmy during their ride. "How are our boys doing?" he demanded. "Is there a chance of stopping this invasion?"

Jimmy told him soberly: "They're not doing so well, Major.

All our peace-lovers—" his voice took on an edge of bitterness— "have practically delivered the country to the mercy of the invaders by hamstringing legislation that would have enabled us to prepare for a thing like this. Almost all of our armament is outmoded. Our pitifully few planes were literally blasted out of the air in the first three days of fighting. Their guns outrange ours two and three times—and even if we should succeed in putting every one of their guns out of commission by sabotage, the way we did with their Big Bertha, they would always have that devilish Green Gas."

Major Fielding swore softly under his breath. "But we have money, wealth, natural resources! We're the richest country on earth—!"

"True! But we haven't spent that money and those resources to build up adequate defenses. The Central Empire has levied taxes until they hurt—has used every cent it could raise—for military purposes. We can't fight guns and gases with money. There's a time when money is no good—and this is the time!"

"Then," Fielding asked brokenly, "there's—no chance for us?"

"It looks bad," Jimmy admitted. "We are hampered in our use of gases, because it could mean the death of all our own people in the occupied territory. The ordinary chemical gases which could be used in war are no good against the Central Empire. Their long-range guns make it possible for them to destroy our defenses from such a distance that the usual gases could not be dispersed far enough to reach them. And even if we did develop a gas as powerful as Maximilian's Green Gas, to use it would mean the destruction of millions of our own people in the occupied territory. Maximilian is clever. He forced his prisoners to remain with the army in great numbers, so that they will be the first to suffer in the event of any determined counterattack."

Jimmy was keeping his eyes on Willfred, watching him closely, for they were passing through a section where the Central Empire troops were concentrated in large numbers. Jimmy frowned. "I wonder what's brought them here in droves! There were very few this morning!"

THEY WERE only a block or two from Bellevue Hospital, and Jimmy ordered Willfred to slow up the horses. He slid down, still keeping the executioner covered. "Get up there, Tim," he ordered the boy. "You've got a gun. Keep it poked in our friend's side. If he yelps, let him have it. I'm going to find out what this is all about."

Tim grinned, swung up on the seat, and produced an automatic from under his blouse. He held it in his lap, pointed toward the executioner. "Look, Willfred," he said. "I hate guys who chop off people's heads. I'd like it swell if I had to shoot you. So the very first yelp you let out—" Tim winked at him significantly—"will be absolutely the last!"

Willfred remained silent, scowling while Diane, the Major and the other prisoners watched Jimmy Christopher swagger over to a Central Empire officer who seemed to be in command of a detail of troops that he was disposing along the riverfront.

The officer saluted as Jimmy approached, glancing respectfully at his staff uniform. He saw the tumbril with its prisoners, and asked: "You come from Execution Square, sir? I heard the firing, and the bugles. Was it an attack?"

Jimmy shrugged. "I could not stay to find out. I must escort these prisoners to safety. What is this activity here?"

The officer pointed to the pile of ruins two blocks north, where Bellevue Hospital had stood. "We have discovered that some Americans have taken refuge there, sir. We do not know who they are, but we suspect that they are of Operator 5's guerrillas. We are preparing to attack them. We will advance from three sides on land, and we are sending a small gunboat up the river to cut off their retreat. We but await the gunboat's appearance to attack!"

"I see," said Jimmy. His body was taut, his mind working swiftly. "How soon will the gunboat be here?"

"In a half hour, sir. It is steaming up from the Battery."

Jimmy turned away with an appearance of carelessness. "Thank you. I will go on with the prisoners."

He returned to the tumbril, climbed up in silence beside Tim and the driver. His face told Diane and the others that he had heard bad news. "Jimmy!" she exclaimed. "What is it?"

He answered her slowly. "They've discovered our hiding place. They're going to attack in a half hour. I have two hundred men quartered in there, and they'll be wiped out!"

FOR A second there was silence. Major Fielding exclaimed: "God, man, what'll you do? We've got to warn them in some way!

"Warning won't do much good. They're outnumbered, in the heart of enemy territory." Jimmy Christopher's eyes met those of Diane Elliot. She said huskily: "Jimmy! There's something else—something you haven't told me. I can see it in your face!"

He nodded. "There *is* something else, Di. Nan is in there, too!" *

Diane's lips trembled. "Nan! But why—?"

"She refused to leave when the others fled from the city. She wanted to make herself useful, so I'm using her as telegraph operator. She's been working the key, communicating with the front lines. Dad is with G.H.Q., and they're using our private code—it's the one code we're sure the enemy can't break down."

Jimmy's eyes were dull. "And it's not only Nan I'm thinking of, Di. It's the boys who're trapped in there. They've all worked with me for the last ten days, risking their lives every minute. I can't let them be destroyed or captured any more than I could

---

* AUTHOR'S NOTE: Readers of some of the early chronicles of the exploits of Operator 5 will recall Jimmy Christopher's beautiful, daring twin sister, Nan Christopher, who was active in assisting her twin brother, often barely escaping with her life. For some time Nan had been traveling in queer corners of the earth, and the experiences which she underwent are a story in themselves, which the author hopes sometime to have the leisure to record. It was only recently that she returned to this country, surfeited with travel and excitement, hoping to retire to a life of quietness. But the invasion of the Purple Emperor smashed her hopes in that direction. Together with Jimmy's father, John Christopher, whom the reader will meet shortly, she entered the lists alongside her twin brother, in the almost hopeless struggle against Maximilian I. Diane Elliot, who loves Nan Christopher perhaps as much as Jimmy does, shares an equal place in his affections, but in a different way. And Diane and Nan are a perfect example of how two girls can love the same man yet not be rivals.

let it happen to Nan or to you. And if they should be wiped out, it would eliminate the only group inside the enemy lines who are armed, and who are in communication with the American forces. It would cut off G.H.Q. from its last source of information. I've *got* to spring them from that trap!"

Suddenly Operator 5 snapped his fingers. There was a reckless light in his eyes that frightened Diane. She knew that look, had seen it in the past when Jimmy Christopher had taken death-defying chances in some mad undertaking. Jimmy swung toward the prisoners, talked to them through the bars of the cage, earnestly, low:

"Are you men willing to take a long shot on rescuing those boys in there? My twin sister is with them, but this is no personal matter with me. You can see the importance of keeping my guerrilla band alive. The attempt may mean death for all of us—"

Major Fielding interrupted him, laughing happily. "I think I can speak for all of us, Operator 5. You don't have to ask whether we are game. Why, if the execution had taken place as scheduled, our heads would be in the basket by now. We're living on borrowed time as it is, and we owe that time to you. Command us, Operator 5!"

Jimmy's eyes glowed warmly. "Thanks, Major, and all of you!" he murmured. "With courage like yours, we can't fail!"

He swung on Willfred, who was sullenly holding the horses' reins, waiting in vain for Tim Donovan to relax his vigilance. "Turn those horses around!" Jimmy ordered. "Drive downtown along the riverfront. And make it snappy. We got away with murder once today. Let's push our luck—while we're lucky!"

CHAPTER 4
ULTIMATUM OF DOOM

A T ABOUT the same time the executioner's sword was poised over Diane Elliot's head in New York that morning, another dramatic scene was being enacted behind the front lines of the American Defense Forces, some four hundred miles away.

The United States troops had dug in the night before, along a line roughly extending south of Lake Erie along the railroad from Toledo through Lima, Dayton and Cincinnati, thence westward to Eagle Mountain and southwestward along the Susquehanna River down to Chesapeake Bay. All the territory east of the Susquehanna was in the hands of Maximilian's forces. And the Americans under General Humphrey hadn't dug their trenches very deep, for they knew they wouldn't be able to hold them long.

General Humphrey had established G.H.Q. at the flying field just outside the town of York, about twenty miles behind the lines. He was the youngest man ever to have been in command of a major American force of troops. Incidentally, he was the fourth man in twenty-two days to be in supreme command. In desperation, the War Office had turned from one man to another, as defeat followed defeat, until the function of the supreme command resolved itself down to the business of managing to keep the retreat as orderly as possible, with the least possible loss of life.

Humphrey was forty-six years old, but he looked sixty. He

had aged that much in the last three days. He was impatiently pacing up and down now, in the operations shack, while a lieutenant at a field telephone rapped questions into the instrument and made rapid notes on a pad. Nearby, an elderly man sat at a telegraph key. He was not operating it, but seemed to be stationed there waiting for it to come to life. This man bore a striking resemblance to Jimmy Christopher himself. He looked very much like an older edition of Operator 5.

He was Q-6, of the United States Intelligence, retired. His name was John Christopher, and he was the father of Operator 5. Owing to a serious wound he had received some years ago, he was no longer in active service, but he often worked with his son, as he was doing now. His job was to receive the code messages which were sent from the hiding place in the powerhouse of the Bellevue Hospital in New York. The code which was used was one which was not known to more than five people in the world—Jimmy Christopher, John Christopher, Tim Donovan, Diane Elliot, and Jimmy's twin sister, Nan.

Humphrey came and stood over Q-6's shoulder, growled: "Any word from Operator 5?"

John Christopher shook his head. "Nothing all morning. He left to perfect his plans for the rescue of Diane. If anything had happened, I'm sure Nan would have buzzed me."

Humphrey grunted, turned to an orderly. "Post a notice. Say that nothing new has occurred with regard to Diane Elliot." He turned back to John Christopher when the orderly had saluted and left. "It's funny," he said, "how our men have taken that plucky girl to their hearts. They idolize her—because she had the guts to buck the Purple Emperor. I almost think that if she should be executed they'd go out and storm the enemy lines with their bare hands!"

Q-6 said fervently: "I hope to God Jimmy succeeds in his plans. That girl is like a daughter to me!"

THE MAN at the field phone arose, brought General Humphrey a sheet of paper upon which he had drawn a rough map, and marked in the position of the enemy troops which he had ascertained from scouts by telephone.

"The enemy hasn't begun today's advance yet, sir. They're still occupying their old positions. I don't understand it!"

Humphrey glanced at the sheet. "Hm!" he muttered. "They must have something up their sleeve. We've left them a clear path to the Susquehanna. They've got nothing to do but march—and they aren't moving!" Suddenly his cheeks blanched. "By God! I wonder if they're going to use their damned gas again!"

He swung on the lieutenant who had given him the map. "Phone the scouts! Have Major Kilbourne send up half a dozen observation crates—even if they get shot out of the air. I've got to know if they intend to use the gas! Let them observe if there's any exceptional activity. My God, if they use the Green Gas now we're in a hell of a hole. I've got two hundred thousand men between here and South Mountain. They'd be slaughtered in an hour!"

The lieutenant hastened back to the field telephone while General Humphrey stood at the door of the shack, peering morosely to the eastward. The York Road, which passed close to the airport, was clogged with infantry. Men in olive drab were plodding silently toward the front line, not singing, not joking, but soberly, like men marching to their certain doom. From all over the country, these men had been rushed to the East, on the theory that manpower would take the place of long-range guns and lethal gases.

Plugger Dugan

But these men knew that the enemy guns could drop a thundering barrage from at least twice or three times the distance their own guns could fire; they knew that the enemy could, at will, release a gas that would wipe them out immediately, against which no type of gas mask yet devised could protect them. They carried masks, yes; and the latest form of respirators. But they had no confidence in them. And with men whose morale had sunk that low, neither General Humphrey nor anyone else could fight a war.

The general's thin, almost ascetic face was drawn into lines of worry as he turned from the doorway in response to the lieutenant's call. The junior officer had his hand over the mouthpiece, and was saying excitedly:

"There's an envoy at the front line, sir, with a flag of truce. He says he has a message for you. Captain Lang wants to know if he should send him on. The messenger refuses to talk to anyone but you."

Humphrey frowned, glanced doubtfully at John Christopher. "A message? If they want us to surrender, by God—"

John Christopher broke in: "Better have him over, General.

There's nothing to lose, and it'll delay the enemy's advance for a while, anyway."

Humphrey nodded. "All right, Stevens. Tell Lang to give the messenger a car and an escort."

TWENTY MINUTES later, a squad car raced up to the shack, and a meticulously dressed, suave Central Empire officer descended from it. He wore the uniform of a major, and he had with him two Central Empire petty officers. He entered the shack, escorted by the detail of American men from the front line, and bowed low, from the hips, to Humphrey.

"I have the honor," he asked, in perfect English, "to address the commander of the American defense forces?"

Humphrey nodded suspiciously. "I am General Humphrey. What is it, sir?"

The officer bowed once more. "Permit that I introduce myself. I am Count Leopold von Hauglein, staff-major in the army of his Imperial Majesty, Maximilian I, Emperor of Europe and Asia. I have a message to deliver to you, sir, by word of mouth, from the generalissimo in command of His Imperial Majesty's Expeditionary Forces."

Humphrey queried, "Yes?"

Count Leopold glanced about distastefully at the staff officers in the shack. There were half a dozen of them, and they were listening keenly to what the Central Empire officer had to say. "Perhaps if we had a bit more of privacy?"

Humphrey nodded, and motioned to the officers, who filed out, except for the lieutenant at the field telephone and for John

Christopher, whom Humphrey motioned to remain. "Now," said the general, "you may give me your message."

Count Leopold showed his even white teeth in a taunting smile. "My message is as follows: You are to understand, General Humphrey, that our generalissimo has it within his discretion to use our Green Gas at any time that he sees fit. Thus far he has refrained from using it except in the state of Maine, for the reason that he does not wish to destroy the entire population of your country. Our glorious Emperor has no wish to conquer a land of corpses!"

Humphrey frowned. "I understand that perfectly. But if you are going to ask us to surrender—"

Count Leopold von Hauglein held up a thin, aristocratic hand. "Not at all, my general. That will come in time, when your countrymen have finally realized the folly of resistance. If you were to surrender at this time, the western and southern portions of your country would not understand that our victory is inevitable. They would think that you had betrayed them, and they would organize their own defenses. We would have the additional task of conquering the country piecemeal. Our plan at this time is to push you back toward the Mississippi. By then, the whole country will understand that it is useless to resist, and they will look with less abhorrence upon the idea of becoming subjects of Maximilian I. Believe me, sir, incredible as it may seem, we do not ask your surrender—yet. Though we have the power to enforce it!"

Humphrey's face was purple, but he restrained himself. "What do you want then?"

Count Leopold smiled deprecatingly. "We are going to make a small—a very modest request—which we are sure will be granted. If you do not grant this request, then we shall, very reluctantly, be compelled to use our Green Gas once more. You have two hundred thousand men on the front lines. There are, perhaps, another two million noncombatants in the surrounding territory. They will all perish when the Green Gas is released—unless our very reasonable request is granted."

"What is that request?" Humphrey asked hoarsely. John Christopher and Lieutenant Stevens hitched forward in their chairs as Count Leopold spoke slowly, carefully: "There is a certain man who has been a thorn in the side of our august emperor. He has carried on guerrilla warfare inside our lines, has disrupted the smooth functioning of the new governments which we are setting up in the occupied territory. Our Emperor has sworn to see this man executed. He is known as Operator 5—"

COUNT LEOPOLD stopped for a moment as Humphrey and John Christopher started at mention of the name, then went on: "This Operator 5 must give himself up before sundown today. We know that he is in touch with you here, from his hiding place in New York. You must order him to give himself up at once to the commandant of the New York area. If he does not do so by sundown, we will release our Green Gas!"

Humphrey was stunned for a moment. Then he exclaimed: "That's impossible! How can we compel Operator 5 to give himself up? He is working independently of us—"

Count Leopold shrugged. "Operator 5 is a man of conscience.

I am sure that if you transmit my message to him, he will be glad to sacrifice himself in order to save a million Americans from the Green Gas."

"But—!"

Leopold raised his hand. "It is useless to argue, General. Those are the terms of His Majesty. There is nothing further to be said. Hostilities will commence again, as usual, as soon as I have returned. No reply is necessary from you. But at sundown, if Operator 5 is still at large, the Green Gas will flood this territory!"

He bowed. "I have the honor, sir, to bid you good-by!" Count Leopold von Hauglein saluted stiffly, spun on his heel, and strode from the shack.

Humphrey and John Christopher exchanged glances. They were silent while they heard the car outside start, then depart with a burst from its exhaust. Then General Humphrey, looking steadily at John Christopher, said: "They'll do it, Q-6. They'll release the Green Gas at sundown if Operator 5 doesn't give himself up. That message must go out to guerrilla headquarters in New York!"

John Christopher's face was gray. "It's my own son!" he said hoarsely. "Jimmy will surely surrender when he gets the message, rather than see more than a million people perish. And God forgive me, I have to be the one to tell him. I have to sentence my own son to death!"

Humphrey lowered his glance before the agony he saw in John Christopher's eyes. He came close, put a rough hand on the older man's shoulder. "It's hell. But you've got to do it, Q-6."

"If I could only go in his place," John Christopher groaned.

Humphrey was silent. There was little that could be said.

Slowly, with a hand that shook a little, and with his lips twisted into a thin, tight line of agony, John Christopher reached out and began to flash the call to Nan Christopher in New York, using their private code:

"N. C.—N. C.—take this carefully, Nan...."

And Humphrey, watching him, gulped hard, turned away, and met the awed glance of Lieutenant Stevens, who had heard the whole thing. "Talk about the old Spartans!" the general muttered. *"That's* what you call—*guts!"*

Outside, from the northeast, came the distant rumble of cannonading. Shells began to shriek about the shack. The marching men on the road outside dispersed, running for cover, as terrific, thunderous detonations tore the earth apart. The air was filled with the whine of catapulting lead, with the smoke and din and thunder of the barrage the enemy was laying down. From behind came the feeble responses of the American gun batteries, ineffectual against the long-range weapons of the Central Empire.

Hell broke loose along the Susquehanna. Overhead, high up, enemy planes filled the sky like locusts, the insignia of the crossed broadswords and the severed head showing on the underside of their wings.

General Humphrey sprang out of the shack, issued staccato orders that sent orderlies and messengers scurrying everywhere. Death screamed from every angle.

But within the shack, a stony-faced man sat at the telegraph

key, regardless of the rain of steel that blanketed the sky, regardless of the death that shrieked at his elbow. He was tapping
out on that key a message that meant he was signing the death
warrant for his own son; and he almost hoped that the frenzied
destruction all about would reach out and encompass him before
he finished....

CHAPTER 5
DEEP-SEA HIJACKERS

BACK IN New York, while that message was being tapped
out, each dot and dash hammering an agonized refrain
at the brain of the man who was sending it, the executioner's tumbril was racing south along the riverfront, with Jimmy
Christopher and Tim Donovan up on the driver's seat beside the
sullen Willfred. The hoofs of the two horses pounded hollowly
on the broken pavement. Diane, Major Fielding and the other
prisoners in the cage stood tensely watching Jimmy Christopher,
while Jimmy, in turn, watched the river. Tim Donovan kept his
eyes on Willfred, pressing his automatic into the executioner's
ribs unobtrusively, so that the patrols they passed suspected
nothing wrong.

They passed Fourteenth Street, and looking eastward along
the wide thoroughfare they could see the cowed crowds of men
and women streaming out of Union Square. At Tim's nudge,
the executioner urged the horses to greater speed as they passed,
lest they be spied by the troops returning from the false alarm.

But at the next corner, Jimmy Christopher suddenly

The impact was like the lash of a whip!

exclaimed: "Hold it, Willfred!" He had spied the burly form of Plugger Dugan racing across Thirteenth Street, toward the river. Plugger was dressed in the fall uniform of a petty officer of the Central Empire. Jimmy had gotten it the day before, when he had made his plans for the rescue of Diane, intending to have one of his own guerrillas use it. But he had taken advantage of Plugger's presence at the library that morning to enlist his services. It was Plugger who had set off the train of firecrackers, and who had vanished at once, making his way across town as soon as he was assured that the troops in Union Square had fallen for the ruse. Now Plugger, grinning like a chimpanzee, climbed aboard the tumbril, clinging to the back step, behind the door.

The tumbril proceeded south, and in a few minutes they passed the ruins of the Williamsburg Bridge, which had been hit early in the bombardment. Its twisted steel girders lay bare and broken on the New York side of the river. In the center, the immense span had fallen completely, leaving a gaping chasm between the struts on this side and those on the Queens side of the stream. Just below the bridge, Jimmy Christopher saw a gunboat steaming along.

Tim Donovan saw it too, and shouted: "There it is, Jimmy! That's the boat that's going to bottle up Nan and the boys in the powerhouse!"

Jimmy nodded. "Here's where we try something ticklish." He ordered Wilfred to stop close to the riverbank, got down, and motioned to Plugger Dugan to join him. The prisoners in the cage had explained the situation to Plugger already, and his fore-head was creased with worry. "What you gonna do?" he asked.

"We're going to capture that ship, Plugger," Jimmy told him calmly. "You and I!"

Plugger stared at him. "You and me? The two of us—capture that battleship?"

"That's what I said!"

Dugan started to laugh, throwing his head back in uproari-ous enjoyment. "Boy, you're tops wit me. I don't know how we're gonna do it—but let's go!"

Jimmy gave him a quick smile, turned and pulled a handker-chief from his pocket, began to wave it toward the gunboat, on whose bridge he could see a small group of officers. The ship was not far from the shore, and the naval officers were looking with curiosity at the tumbril full of prisoners, and at the young man in the uniform of the Emperor's staff officer who was waving to them.

JIMMY SAW one of the officers go into the cabin behind the bridge and emerge almost at once with a man who was evidently the captain, from the quantity of gold braid flung across his uniform. The captain gazed toward the shore curi-ously, and Jimmy renewed the urgency with which he waved the handkerchief. For a breathless moment he did not know whether the captain would rise to the bait, but he sighed with relief as he saw the captain nod and turn back into the cabin, closing the door behind him.

The officer who had called him saluted the captain's depart-ing back, lifted a speaking tube from the rack on the bridge, and

spoke an order to the engine room.
The ship had almost passed the spot
on the shore where Jimmy Christopher and Plugger Dugan stood, when
she suddenly began to churn water
forward in response to the officer's
command.

Plugger Dugan squeezed Jimmy's
arm. "She's stopping, Cap! She's stopping!"

They watched while a boat was
lowered and, with an officer and eight
men manning it, rowed toward the
shore.

Jimmy said to Dugan out of the corner of his mouth: "Now
you keep absolutely still, Plugger. Say nothing and do nothing,
till I tell you. Remember, you're a petty officer of His Imperial
Majesty, Maximilian I, and I'm a staff officer. Be respectful to
me and to the gunboat's commander—till I tell you to be otherwise."

"Don't worry, Cap," Plugger Dugan said. "I'll keep mum. I
don't see yet how you figger to grab the ship. But you tell me
what to do, an' I'll do it!"

Officers and crew lined the rope rail of the low, rakish
gunboat, as the dinghy pulled in alongside the small jetty near
the shore. Jimmy Christopher walked out on the jetty as the
officer in charge climbed out. Jimmy addressed him at once,
speaking the guttural, native tongue of the other:

"I regret to inconvenience you, but it is the Emperor's wish that these prisoners whom I have here be conducted aboard your ship at once. If you will be so good as to bring me to your commanding officer, I shall explain the circumstances to him."

The officer was very evidently impressed by Jimmy Christopher's staff uniform. He cast a curious glance at the tumbril, with the executioner and Tim Donovan in the driver's seat, then saluted smartly. "Step into the boat, Captain," he said to Jimmy.

Operator 5 motioned to Dugan to follow, and stepped into the dinghy, aided by the officer. They were swiftly rowed to the gunboat, and escorted up to the bridge, Dugan following Jimmy at a respectful distance, as a staff officer's orderly should do.

The gunboat's captain was standing at the door of his cabin, and he eyed Operator 5 questioningly. Jimmy assumed the arrogance of tone which a favorite of the Emperor might use, said to the captain:

"Your name and rank, sir?"

The captain, a straight-backed, gaunt-faced man with the traditional student's dueling scar across his left cheek, frowned for a moment, then replied with a touch of contempt:

"I am Sub-Commandant Ellberg, at the Emperor's service. What is it that you wish?"

"May I see you in the privacy of your cabin for but a second?"

"Of course."

The sub-commandant bowed, stood aside for Jimmy to enter, then followed him, closing the door and leaving Plugger Dugan outside.

ELLBERG FACED Jimmy Christopher coldly, said: "You

will be good enough to make your request quickly. We are on our way to aid in the attack upon a nest of American guerrillas which has been discovered further up the river—"

"Certainly," Jimmy said crisply. "I merely want you to take aboard my load of prisoners."

"I am sorry. But that cannot be done. If you have an order from the Emperor, or from Baron zu Lambrecht—?"

"I have this!" Jimmy said softly. He stepped in close, brought up his bunched fist in a short, swift blow to the side of Captain Ellberg's jaw. The *snap* of that impact cracked like the lash of a whip. And Ellberg's eyes changed abruptly from surprised consternation to a vacant stare. He crumpled slowly and lay in a heap on the cabin floor.

Jimmy moved swiftly now. He stooped and pulled the unconscious man over to one side, then opened the door of the cabin and faced the officers on the bridge. Dugan was standing there, shifting from one foot to the other, completely at sea. Those men had been talking to him in their native language, and he did not understand a word of what they said. Therefore he had made no answer. They were growing suspicious, and Dugan looked helplessly at Jimmy.

Operator 5 paid no attention to him, however. He said to the officers:

"Gentlemen, I have taken over command of this ship in the name of the Emperor. You will take your orders from me!"

The officer who had brought them over in the dinghy took a startled step forward. "But, Excellency, what of Commander Ellberg—?"

"He has been temporarily relieved of command," Jimmy informed him coldly. "And now you will at once proceed to lower boats and pick up those prisoners from the tumbril."

The officer hesitated. "Your Excellency, I am Oberleutnant Forstner, the second in command of this ship. If the captain has done anything to displease the Emperor, then I should automatically take com—"

"You will automatically remain second in command, Herr Forstner. Please carry out my orders at once!"

Forstner demurred. "Could I ask to see your authority, Excellency—"

"Certainly," Jimmy said pleasantly. "Here it is!"

His automatic abruptly appeared in his hand, trained on Forstner's abdomen. "Does this convince you?"

There were three other officers on the bridge besides Forstner, and none of them was a coward. They scowled, and one of them took a quick step to one side, his hand going to his holster. Another stepped to the left. Their intention was to flank Jimmy Christopher. One, possibly two of them might be shot by him, but the others would surely get Jimmy Christopher. However, they had forgotten to take Plugger Dugan into consideration. It was a fatal mistake on their part.

Plugger swung into action with blinding speed. A sledgehammer blow to the side of the head brought one of them down in a heap. Dugan didn't stop. He swung around like a whirlwind, and gripped a second man by the arm, twisted hard, and the arm snapped like a reed, forcing the squealing cry of a stuck pig from the stricken man. Jimmy Christopher had stepped into the fray, his eyes bright with the excitement of action. The barrel of his automatic came down in a smashing blow, shattering the wrist of Oberleutnant Forstner, causing him to drop the revolver he had pulled from his holster. The fourth officer sprang backward, snarling, swinging his gun at Plugger Dugan. But Jimmy launched himself at this man, in a flying tackle which sent him crashing to the floor, jarring the revolver from his grip. The man's head struck a stanchion, and he stiffened, his arms spread-eagling, blood streaming from a deep cut behind his ear....

JIMMY PICKED himself up, grinned at Plugger Dugan, who was wiping his hands on his uniform and blowing on his knuckles. The crew, down below on the deck, trained in the thoroughgoing, strict discipline of the Central Empire Navy, had not even cast a glance up at the bridge, and were unaware of the battle that had just taken place there.

Plugger Dugan cast a glance of admiration at Jimmy. "Well, Cap, I gotta say you got guts! Who'd've had the nerve to make a play like this? What do we do next?"

"Get those birds in the cabin," Jimmy ordered swiftly, "and strip them. Then lock them in a closet or something. We'll be able to use their uniforms for what we have to do!"

Jimmy went forward on the bridge, issued swift orders to the crew below. They, accustomed as they were to unquestioning obedience to an officer's commands, hastened to obey. Two boats were launched, and Jimmy descended, entered one of them. Plugger Dugan remained in charge of the bridge.

Ashore, Jimmy superintended the unloading of the amazed prisoners from the tumbril. Willfred, the executioner, opened his mouth to shout to the sailors, but Tim Donovan, who had stuck with him, dug the gun viciously into the man's ribs, and he quieted. Jimmy ordered two of the seamen: "Take that man straight up on the bridge. He is not to talk, understand? If he opens his mouth to make one sound, you will shoot him!"

The sailors saluted respectfully. They swung their rifles to cover the executioner, pushed him ahead toward the boat. Will-fred's face was a study in frustration. He had watched the boats approaching, as he sat in the driver's seat of the tumbril and had expected that that would be his opportunity to denounce the impostor, whom he now knew to be Operator 5. But he kept a discreet silence. He was familiar enough with the discipline of the Central Empire navy to know that the seamen would liter-ally obey Jimmy Christopher's order. He had only to open his mouth to have the two rifles bark behind him, to receive the impact of two slugs in his liver. So he kept silence.

Jimmy returned in the same boat with Diane and Major Fielding, but he did not talk to them. It was imperative for the success of his plans that the sailors should suspect nothing.

Tim Donovan rode in the other boat, with the executioner, as an additional precaution against his blabbing. The boy had taken Willfred's immense sword along, and held it across his knees, careful that the razor sharp edge did not cut him.

Aboard the ship, the prisoners ascended to the bridge under the surprised gaze of the seamen, who had thought that they were to be stowed below. Willfred was brought along, and Plug-ger Dugan locked him up in the linen closet with the officers whom he had stripped of their uniforms.

Jimmy Christopher issued a series of orders to the engine room, and the gunboat got under weigh once more. The capture of the ship had been unbelievably simple, as all daring undertakings usually are. No one on shore suspected that the *Regina*, as they discovered the vessel's name to be, was not under the control of its regular officers.

In order to continue this illusion, Jimmy had Major Fielding and three other men from among the prisoners don the uniforms which Dugan had taken from the men in the linen closet. Once more the bridge was occupied by swaggering officers of the Imperial Navy of His Majesty, Maximilian I, Emperor of Europe and Asia. But Maximilian was far from pleased when he learned of the next steps taken by those officers....

CHAPTER 6
THE SIEGE OF BELLEVUE

THE POWERHOUSE of Bellevue Hospital was a fairly large structure, accommodating fairly comfortably the more than two hundred men who made up Operator 5's guerrilla band. Strangely, by some quirk of fate, the bombardment of the city had destroyed all the ward buildings, killing hundreds of patients, tumbling them in ruins over the crushed bodies of the sick and those who had been ministering to them; yet it had spared the one building which could be used against the invaders.

For the dynamo had furnished power which Jimmy Christopher had used in devious ways. One night that week, he had strung two miles of wire through the city streets to the ammunition stores which the Central Empire army had stowed in the General Post Office Building on Thirty-third Street. Fifty of his men had aided in the undertaking, laying the wire through back yards, dodging patrols, stealing through the night. Then, when everything was set, Jimmy had shot a charge of electric current through that wire which had sent the Post Office Building, together with countless stores of ammunition and high explosive, high into the air in a rending explosion.

Then, under cover of the panic and excitement which followed, they had picked up the wire, eliminating all trace of the agency which had caused it!

So far, the band had successfully kept their hiding-place a secret. The debris of the hospital buildings was piled high in the acre of land that Bellevue had occupied. To an observer from the street, it seemed that there was nothing here worth investigating. But to make sure that they would not be caught napping, Jimmy Christopher had posted men on the street side and on the riverfront. Within, machine guns and grenades were ready to hand. These were of the very latest type, having been looted from trucks of the Central Empire. The men were all determined that, in the event of discovery, they would sell their lives as dearly as possible. The powerhouse was not the ideal hiding-place, but it was the best they had been able to find so far. It would have to do.

Up on the balcony which ran around the interior of the building a table had been set up, upon which a makeshift telegraph set was in operation. At the key sat a bright-eyed young lady whose blonde hair framed her lively face in soft waves. She bore a remarkable resemblance to Operator 5. She was, in fact, his twin sister, Nan Christopher. Beside her stood a diminutive man of perhaps forty, entirely bald, with small, shrewd eyes, and hands whose long, supple fingers might have been those of an artist—or a pickpocket!

This man was smoking a cigarette, puffing it nervously, swiftly. At his feet on the floor there was a small pile of butts, attesting to the number of cigarettes he had already consumed. This man was Slips McGuire, a gentleman who had been a pickpocket until Jimmy Christopher took him in hand. Jimmy had recognized the innate redeeming qualities of Slips McGuire, had expended the time and the effort to make him a useful citizen. And Operator 5 now had no more loyal adherent than the little ex-pickpocket.

Now, he was saying anxiously: "Gosh, Miss Christopher, why hasn't your brother come back yet? He only went out to spot the lay o' the land, and to look at the notices at the library. An' here he is, gone over two hours. You think something's happened to him?"

NAN CHRISTOPHER, unlike Diane, was not the type who worried much. She smiled at McGuire, toying with the telegraph key. "If you knew Jimmy as well as I know him, Slipsy," she said, "you wouldn't worry about him. He has a charmed life. He'll live to be a hundred and ten. And when he does die and goes to hell, he'll be too tough for the boys down there, and they'll send him right back."

Slips grinned at her. "Gosh, Miss Christopher, you're a regular girl, ain't you? I bet you was a tomboy when you was a kid."

Nan laughed, her fresh young voice sounding musically in the semidark building. She glanced down at the main floor, where the bulk of Jimmy's band were lounging about at tables, on improvised chairs, and on the floor. They were playing cards in the dim light—they could not risk too much light, for fear of detection, and the windows were very high up, so that little sunlight filtered in—or idly chatting. Near the two doors, one facing east, the other west, were racks of machine guns and rifles, and to one side of them were sacks of grenades. Many of the men were perched upon the huge dynamo in the center of the floor, which rose above the balcony, so that those who sat on it were above the level of Nan Christopher's seat.

Nan, watching these men, detected a little overtone of uneasiness in their voices. None of them was saying it, but all shared Slips McGuire's worry about Jimmy Christopher's failure to return. And there was also Tim Donovan, who had often cheered them up on a dull evening with his Irish sauciness and kid tricks.

One of the men on the dynamo called out to her: "You been in touch with G.H.Q. lately, Nan?"

She shook her head. "There's nothing to report, and I don't feel like telling Dad that Jimmy hasn't come back yet—" She stopped as the key under her hands came to life. A sudden tenseness fell over the big place, as they all realized that a message was coming in from G.H.Q. Daily now, they had been getting reports of constant retreat, of the destruction of more and more men in one-sided battle. They almost feared to hear more.

Nan wrote busily as the key clicked, taking down the code

which John Christopher was tapping out four hundred miles away. The message finished, and Nan clicked out an acknowledgment, then set about deciphering it.

Suddenly, as the meaning of the message began to come to her, she uttered a short gasp, and her hand began to shake. The point of her pencil broke, and she reached unsteadily for another, went on automatically decoding the balance.

Slips McGuire asked her quickly:

"What's up, Miss Christopher?" She didn't answer, and he bent over, read the words her pencil was forming:

TELL JIMMY WE HAVE JUST RECEIVED ULTIMATUM FROM CENTRAL EMPIRE... MAXIMILIAN WANTS HIM BADLY AND THREATENS TO RELEASE GREEN GAS IN THIS ENTIRE TERRITORY UNLESS JIMMY GIVES HIMSELF UP BEFORE SUNDOWN TONIGHT... OVER ONE MILLION PEOPLE WILL DIE IF GAS IS RELEASED... NAN I HATE MYSELF FOR TRANSMITTING MESSAGE BUT YOU MUST TELL JIMMY... WISH TO GOD I COULD GO IN HIS PLACE....

Slips McGuire let out a deep sigh as he finished reading the last word. "Gawd!" he said under his breath. "That devil

Maximilian! It puts Jimmy in a spot!" He clutched Nan's arm. "Don't tell him, Miss Christopher. If you tell him, he'll surely give himself up!"

Nan's voice was wracked by a sob as she answered. "But how can I not tell him, Slips? He'd never forgive me if I let a million people die that way. Did you see how they look after the gas gets them? They're all bloated up and purple. It's—horrible!" Her red lips quivered. "If Jimmy—!"

SHE WAS interrupted by shouts from the men down below, and on the dynamo. "What's the message, Nan? Is it bad? Come on, give it to us. We can take it—by this time!"

Nan groaned: "Slips, I can't tell him. I—won't!" She buried her head in her arms on the table.

The shouts were renewed, impatiently. These men were starved for news. Many had relatives, sons and brothers in the front lines and in the territory where the fighting was taking place. They wanted to know what was happening. "Come on, Nan! Give us the dope! Dish it out. Is it that bad?"

Slips McGuire turned on them, shouting: "Damn you, shut up! It's—something personal. Forget it! Can't you see how bad Miss Christopher feels? Leave her alone!"

The calls subsided. The men liked Nan a lot, and they had developed a healthy respect for the little ex-pickpocket. They grumbled a little, but gave up their efforts.

And just then the door was pushed open, and the guard who had been stationed outside burst in. He was a young chap, hardly more than nineteen, with a smooth face and rosy cheeks that were beginning to be a little pinched with hunger, as were the cheeks of everyone there; for it was becoming increasingly diffi-cult during the last few days to secure food by foraging. The army had taken charge of rationing, and food was extremely scarce. It had been necessary to raid the army stores only the other day, in order to feed the band. Now, however, all thought of food was gone from the young guard.

His eyes shone with alarm as he blurted out loud: "Boys! I think we're spotted. There's troops gathering on three sides of the building!"

Men, suddenly alert, ran to gather about him. Others climbed by ladders to the high windows to peer out. The quiet atmo-sphere of the place was suddenly gone.

The youthful guard continued to blurt: "They're pulling machine guns into place along the street. No wonder the chief couldn't get back here. The streets are full of soldiers!"

Nan Christopher and Slips McGuire had been too preoccu-pied at first with the message from John Christopher to under-stand the meaning of the guard's announcement. Now, however, Slips said to her tensely, "Miss Christopher! Listen to what he's sayin'! We're gonna be attacked!"

They looked down from the balcony at the scene of bustling activity. Sub-machine guns and hand grenades were being passed out. There was an air of desperate determination among the entire band. One of them raised his arm, shouted: "Well, boys, it looks like the end. We'll give 'em hell before they wipe us out, though!"

There was a chorus of acclamation to that. None of them exhibited any fear or regret. They were fiercely ready to die.

But Nan sprang up, leaned over the railing of the balcony, and called down to them. Her pretty face was flushed, and her hands clenched, one of them clutching the decoded message she had just taken over the key. At first her voice was lost in the general excitement, but after a moment someone shouted: "Hey, boys! Quiet! Miss Christopher wants to say something!"

A hush descended upon them, and Nan seized the chance, speaking swiftly: "If we're going to be attacked, you've got to remember what Operator 5 has often told you—don't fight unless you have to, because the odds are too great against us. It's very brave and noble to put up a good fight, but you've got to remember that we're the only link between this side of the enemy lines and our own G.H.Q. If this outfit is—destroyed, G.H.Q. will be left without any sources of information!"

She let that sink in, then: "We owe it to the country, if not to ourselves, to make every effort to escape before fighting. Let's see if they've got the riverside covered. If they haven't, we might succeed in getting over to Queens."

THE MEN nodded among themselves, recognizing the wisdom of what she proposed. Several of the men who had assumed the mantle of leadership in Operator 5's absence looked shame-faced. They realized that they should have thought of the river. The guard on that side had not appeared, as yet, to give any alarm.

While the arms were being distributed, two men went out on that side to investigate, reported that though they could see soldiers gathering on the streets above and below, there seemed to be nothing to stop them from crossing over into Queens.

"Of course," one of them said, "they could try to pick us off while we were scooting across, but our powerboats are pretty fast. We've got six boats under the tarpaulins alongside the dock. Each one'll hold thirty men at a pinch. They might knock off one or two boats, but the rest'll get across!"

Nan said: "That's a better chance than trying to defend this place. This is a deathtrap. We might be able to stand them off for a while, but we couldn't keep them off forever." She detailed a dozen men to go down to the dock, a distance of less than fifty feet. Almost naturally, now, she had taken the leadership. "You twelve men," she directed, "go and rip the tarps off the boats, prime the engines, and get them ready to start. We'll be coming after you, a few at a time, so there'll be as little chance as possible of their noticing us from the street. If—"

She was interrupted by a cry from one of the men at the rear door. He was pointing out toward the river, shouting: "A gunboat! There's a gunboat coming up. They've got us bottled!"

Nan's heart sank, and she threw a hopeless glance at Slips McGuire, who was standing beside her on the balcony. She went and peered through the window, saw the long, sleek gunboat, with the white flag at the stern upon which there appeared in black the sign of the crossed broadswords and the severed head—the flag of the Central Empire!

One of the men from below—Joe Flagler by name—called up to her: "That's the end of that, Nan. We've got to fight it out. Maybe you could get away while we—"

She shook her head impatiently. "All right, boys. I guess this powerhouse will be our tomb. Take your positions—the way

69

Operator 5 planned for us in case of attack. We'll make it interesting for them, anyway!"

A small group of men moved a machine gun over to the west door, set it up in position, commanding the field of debris and ruins over which the attack would have to come. Others prepared a small pile of grenades. The interior of the powerhouse became a scene of bustle and activity, with an air of grim determination over it all. Nan stood on the balcony, clutching that message which she was sure now she would never be able to deliver to Operator 5. And she wondered whether this wasn't the easiest way out of the dilemma. Now she wouldn't have to tell Jimmy

Men on the dynamo were picking off the advancing gray troops!

that he had to give himself up at sundown. Maybe a million people would perish—but the dreadful decision would be taken out of her hands. She caught Slips McGuire looking at her queerly, and she knew that the same thought was in his mind.

And then, one of the men at the machine gun called out: "Here they come!"

Joe Flagler, an ex-World War veteran, who limped a little on his right leg from an old wound, had taken command of the machine-gun crew. He ordered them: "Hold your fire till they're bunched a little more. Then give it to 'em!"

All of these men were grim. They had no expectation of leaving this place alive. They might hold off the attack for an hour, two, or maybe three hours; but they were bound to lose. Two hundred men with short rations and limited ammunition cannot hold off an army. And they knew that the gunboat in the river could blast them all off the map with a single well-placed shot. But they prepared to fight in tight silence, while the balance of the band fingered rifles and sub-machine guns, ready to back up the crew at the door.

SLIPS McGUIRE was putting a clip in his automatic, and Nan was watching tautly with one hand at her throat. She could see out the door, could see the gray-uniformed Central Empire troops deploying outside in open formation, could see them closing up as they moved in toward the powerhouse.

And Joe Flagler suddenly called out in the deep silence: "Now, boys! Open up!"

The gunners bent, and just then there was the deep-throated detonation of a cannon from somewhere out behind the advancing troops. A short, whining sound, and the whole front of the powerhouse seemed to have been obliterated. The enemy had placed a shot right square on that machine gun. The west wall crumbled in the din of the terrific explosion. Smoke and fumes enveloped the spot where the crew had stood. The machine gun disappeared. Joe Flagler and the dozen or so men who had been crowding at the doorway were blown to bits. A wide opening in the wall yawned where they had been, above a craterlike chasm in the floor.

And from outside came a victorious shout as the gray-clad troops rushed in.

Within the powerhouse the defenders began to fire their rifles and sub-machine guns. Slips McGuire cursed, and leaped from the balcony across to the top of the dynamo, seized one of the rifles that had been stacked there, and lay flat on his stomach, sighting at the attacking troops outside. The bark of rifles, the chatter of quick-firers, smoke and confusion filled the building. The enemy were shooting now too, and men were dropping all over, on the floor.

A withering blast of fire filled the opening which the shell had blasted in the wall. The firing was coming from two machine guns which the attackers had moved up along the flanks, and their crossfire mowed down the defenders. Then a gray wave stormed in through the opening, leaping the chasm at the doorway. Rifles exploded in men's faces, men went down with bayonets in their throats and stomachs.

The gun crew stationed at the east doorway, overlooking the river, had swung their machine gun around to cover the interior of the building, for no attack seemed to be coming from the river. But they could not shoot now, for the building was filled with friend and foe, struggling in tight groups around the four sides of the dynamo, slipping in their own and their enemies' blood.

Slips McGuire and fifteen or twenty other men were perched on top of the dynamo, coolly picking off gray shapes down below. Men's shouts, curses, screams filled the air, mingling with the sharp, quick reports of the rifles. And over it all, Nan Christopher suddenly became conscious that the radio key behind her had come to life.

She leaped to it, and took the message that came clicking over, while smoke and powder filled her eyes. And as she got the tenor of the message, color came into her face, and her eyes sparkled with new hope, mingled with amazement. The message read:

NAN... GET BOYS OUT OF POWERHOUSE... HAVE CONTROL OF GUNBOAT... COME ABOARD....

The message ended with Jimmy Christopher's code signature. Nan didn't question the miracle, but accepted it. How her twin brother had gotten control of the gunboat which was coming up the river, she could no more understand than she had been able at the moment to understand some of the other miraculous things that Operator 5 had accomplished. She only knew now that she must get these boys out of the powerhouse; make them stop fighting, get them a moment's respite from the desperate attack which was rendering the powerhouse into a bloody shambles.

SHE LEANED over, called urgently to Slips McGuire, motioned to him to come to her. Slips stopped shooting, started to scramble across the top of the dynamo. A gray-uniformed soldier down below saw Nan's blonde head over the railing, raised his rifle to fire at her. McGuire, setting himself to leap the intervening space between the dynamo and the balcony, spotted the soldier, yelled and fired at the same time. The soldier's shot went wild, the man crumpled with McGuire's slug through the top of his skull. Immediately his prone body was trampled by madly fighting, squirming men.

McGuire jumped over and Nan quickly showed him the message. Slips, dazed, couldn't understand for a moment. "B-but—how could that be, Miss Christopher? You sure it ain't a trap—?"

"No, no, Slips! It was Jimmy's code signature. We've got to stop the fighting down there. Those troops are going to get reinforcements soon. Every single one of our boys will be slaughtered if we don't get them aboard the ship—"

"I got it!" McGuire exclaimed.

He leaped to the huge panel of switches along the wall. They were the switches that controlled all the dynamo connections, that had originally been used to throw power into every one of the hospital buildings. He seized one of the switches, reaching up on his toes to it, and, turning so that he was facing the fighting below, he emitted a weird sort of shriek that caught and held the attention of the desperate men. Then he shouted at the top of his lungs: "We're licked, boys! I'm gonna touch off the dynamite! Well take all these guys with us to Kingdom Come!"

While the Americans watched him, uncomprehending, one of the Central Empire soldiers who understood English caught his meaning, screamed to his fellows in their native tongue: "He is about to explode dynamite! We will all be blown up! Flee! Flee!"

And the man set an example by launching himself headlong through the door. The panic spread. In a moment, the jagged opening in the wall was jammed with Central Empire troops in gray, struggling to escape the doom that these desperate men were visiting on themselves.

Nan Christopher leaned far over the railing, shouted down: "Out the back way, boys! For God's sake, quick! Make for the boats! My brother has captured the gunboat!"

It took the Americans only a moment to grasp the situation. While the Central Empire soldiers flocked in panic out one exit, Nan's boys started in the other direction, shouting joyfully, carrying their sub-machine guns, rifles and grenades along with them. Slips and Nan ran to the end of the balcony and down the steps, joined the others at the east doorway.

In a moment they were outside, racing toward the power-boats which had been made ready by the men whom Nan had sent out previously.

Before the officers of the Central Empire fully comprehended the ruse, six boats were launched, and were chugging frantically toward the long, trim gunboat in the river.

Even then, the Central Empire troops did not fire upon the fugitives. Their officers thought that the Americans were trapped. They expected every moment to see tongues of flame licking from the portholes of the battleship, and to see the boats smashed out of the water.

Thus, the fugitives reached the ship and climbed the ladders onto the deck, and even then the attackers on land did not realize that they had been cheated of their prey. They cheered, thinking perhaps that the Americans had surrendered and were being taken prisoner on board. Under their very eyes the gunboat executed gracefully the difficult feat of turning around in the river, and steamed south again in a leisurely manner.

A hundred and ten of the original two hundred men in the band were aboard her. The other ninety lay dead on floor of the powerhouse—with an even greater number of Central Empire troops beside them.

Majestically the gunboat made its way down the river, unmolested. No one on the shore suspected even yet that it was in the hands of the daring guerrilla, Operator 5. The delivery had gone off like clockwork, and with the smoothness of well-oiled machinery....

CHAPTER 7
PLUGGER DUGAN SCHEMES

JIMMY CHRISTOPHER stood on the bridge, taut and poised, watching the fugitives from the powerhouse come on board. Beside him were Major Fielding and the other men whom he had dressed in the uniforms of the Central Empire Navy. Inside the cabin Diane Elliot and Tim Donovan watched breathlessly.

Behind them, clustered close together, with whatever weapons they had been able to break out of the stores, were the other prisoners.

Jimmy said to Major Fielding: "This is going to be the ticklish part of it, Major." His eyes were following the course of the second boat, where he could discern Nan's lovely face, flushed with excitement. "Our Central Empire crew doesn't know what this is all about. So far they aren't suspicious. They are wondering why I had the prisoners from the tumbril brought up here but don't dare say anything. They think I've taken over the ship in the name of the Emperor. Now, when these boys come on board, they're liable to suspect that everything isn't according to Hoyle."

Major Fielding laughed. "After the way things have been happening today, I don't think anything you tried could fail, Operator 5!"

Plugger Dugan, who was standing directly behind them, grinned and said: "They ought to make you the boss of the army, Cap. I bet you could win this war in no time, an' drive Mr. Maximilian clear out into the ocean!"

Jimmy didn't answer. The fugitives were almost all aboard, and the crew of the battleship were clustered around them down on the deck. A petty officer looked up to the bridge at Jimmy for orders, called out:

"These men are all armed, Excellency. Shall we take their arms away from them?"

Jimmy leaned over, and spoke in English. He appeared to be talking to the petty officer, but he was really talking to Nan and the other fugitives. "Spread out," he was saying. "Get some distance between yourselves and the crew. You outnumber them three to one—the ones on deck. When I give the word, cover them!"

The petty officer had listened, puzzled. Now he said: "But I do not understand, Excellency. You speak in a language—"

He never finished. The fugitives from the powerhouse had obeyed Jimmy even while he was talking. They formed a wide semicircle, and suddenly the petty officer stopped talking, his jaw dropping open. In a hundred hands, rifles and sub-machine guns were leveled at himself and those of the crew who were on deck. The crew were caught flatfooted. They had received no orders from the bridge to supply themselves with weapons. All but the petty officers were unarmed. They were helpless.

Jimmy called out to them: "You will surrender to these men. Make no resistance. You have no chance at all!"

In less than three minutes, the crew who had been on deck were huddled together under a guard of five men from the powerhouse. A low cheer went up from Jimmy's guerrilla band, but Jimmy hushed it. He called down to them: "Your work isn't done yet. There's the rest of the crew—the engine-room and the gun crews. Spread out over the ship. Make prisoners of all you meet, except those in the engine room. Place a guard over the engineer and his assistants, and keep them on the job. Any of you who know how to navigate, come up here on the bridge. We've got our own navy now!"

THE MEN down on the deck spread out all over the ship, carrying out Jimmy's orders. Nan Christopher raced up the companion ladder, and threw herself into her twin brother's arms. "Jimmy!" she gasped. "How did you do it? We thought we were all through back there in the powerhouse!"

Jimmy squeezed her hard, gave her a resounding kiss, and turned to shake hands with Slips McGuire, who had followed her up.

Diane came out of the cabin, and she and Nan embraced each other, while Tim Donovan danced around behind them, waiting for his chance at Nan.

The engine-room telegraph rang and Jimmy picked it up. He heard one of his own men speaking. "We've got control of the ship, Operator 5, and the engine room is ours!"

"Okay," Jimmy said crisply. "We've got to head back." He superintended the complicated business of turning around in the river, while Tim Donovan introduced Nan and Slips McGuire to Plugger Dugan.

Diane said: "Nan, what's the matter with you? You look quiet, thoughtful. I've never seen you like that. Are you sick?"

Nan looked up at Diane. "No, Di," she said huskily. "I'm not—sick, bodily. I'm sick—at the thought of what I've got to tell Jimmy!"

The others crowded around her. "What do you mean?"

She threw a cautious glance over her shoulder. Jimmy Christopher was busy arranging for the smooth running of the ship they had taken over. He was assigning duties to the various members of the band and to the released prisoners from the tumbril. He paid no attention for the moment to the little group around Nan and Diane, consisting of Tim, Plugger Dugan and Slips McGuire.

Nan said hastily: "Come into some cabin where we can talk. There's something I've got to tell you—before I tell Jimmy."

Tim Donovan threw her a queer glance, but he said: "We can go in the executive officer's cabin. No one's using it right now."

He led the way. Jimmy Christopher didn't notice them leave....

In the executive officer's cabin, Nan burst out without preliminaries: "Here! Read this—" she extended the crumpled paper upon which she had decoded the message from John Christopher—"It came from Dad just before we were attacked!"

Diane took the paper from her, read aloud, and her cheeks blanched as she read. When she had finished there was a short silence in the cabin, broken by Tim Donovan's labored breathing.

Plugger Dugan was the first to speak. "Hey!" he shouted, as he at last understood the full implication of the words Diane had read. "That means that Operator 5 has got to go and surrender himself today! And Maximilian will have his head chopped off!"

Slips McGuire looked up at him scornfully. "That's smart of you, big fella. Did you figger it all out for yourself?"

Dugan reddened. Alongside of the diminutive Slips, he looked like a mighty giant. "Don't get funny, midget!" he growled. "Or I'll take you apart, like I'd take apart my watch, to see what makes it tick!"

Slips McGuire backed away from him, bristling. "Listen, you big baboon," he piped, "you haven't even got the right time, let alone a watch. If you got a watch, let's see it!"

Plugger Dugan put a hand unconsciously to the watch pocket

of his uniform under the tunic. He found it empty. "Hell!" he muttered. "That's funny! I had a watch in there—"

"Maybe this is it?" Slips asked, grinning, and handed him a gold watch and fob.

Dugan grabbed it. "Say! How did you get it?"

Tim Donovan burst out laughing, and Diane and Nan couldn't help joining him, at sight of the ludicrous expression of Plugger Dugan's face. Slips was smirking in self-satisfied fashion. "The hand is quicker than the eye, my friend," he said. "You might have big paws, but I got long fingers."

Diane explained to Plugger: "Slips used to be—er—"

"A pickpocket," Slips finished for her, saving her from her evident embarrassment. You don't have to be bashful about sayin' it, Miss Elliot. It ain't what a guy used to be that counts—it's what he is now. And Operator 5's made a man outta me. An' I ain't takin' guff from this big baboon—"

"Never mind that now," Tim cut in. "You're forgetting about this ultimatum. What'll we do? If we tell Jimmy about it, he'll surely give himself up—he isn't going to let a million people be gassed to save his own skin—"

"And if I don't tell him," Nan broke in, "and those people are gassed, Jimmy'd never forgive me." She swung to Diane, put out an appealing hand. There was a catch in her voice. "Di! Tell me what to do! You—"

"Tell you what to do about what?"

NAN FROZE. In their preoccupation they hadn't heard the door open. Jimmy Christopher stood, eyeing them queerly. It was he who had spoken. He stepped into the cabin. "Excuse me," he said. "I was looking for one of you to take over the wireless. They told me you'd all come in here. I didn't know I was intruding."

He looked from one strained face to the other. "Whose funeral is it?"

Diane managed an artificial, hollow laugh. "Nobody's, Jimmy. Plugger was just telling us a joke."

"Yeah," said Jimmy Christopher. "It must have been an awful funny one—about an undertaker." Coolly he stepped forward, took the crumpled paper from Diane's unresisting fingers. She made no effort to stop him, but her breathing became quicker. Nan uttered an involuntary little gasp. Tim looked distressed, and Plugger Dugan and Slips McGuire lowered their eyes.

There was utter silence in the cabin while Jimmy Christopher read the message from his father, telling him that he would have to give himself up before sundown. Then he raised his eyes. They were inscrutable. "You were going to hold this out on me?"

Nan avoided his glance. "I—I don't know what I was going to do."

Jimmy went on steadily. "If you hadn't given me this, and the Central Empire released the Green Gas tonight, and a million men and women perished—bloated, purpled, distorted—would you ever have been able to forgive yourself? Even though you kept silent for my sake? Would you have been able to sleep nights, with those men and women haunting you? And do you think I would ever have forgiven you?"

Nan choked, gulped, one hand at her breast. She didn't answer.

Silently, Jimmy turned and strode from the cabin.

Diane called after him: "Jimmy! What are you going to do? Are—are you going to give yourself—up?"

He turned and faced her for a second. His eyes were cold and resolved. "What do *you* think, Di?" he asked levelly. And before she could answer, he was gone…!

The door slammed behind him with a strange finality. And Nan cried piteously: "We've got to *do* something! We can't let him go—"

Plugger Dugan interrupted her. His forehead was corrugated with the great effort of thinking. He said: "Listen, folks, I think I got an idea. I think I know a way outta this!"

They all gathered around him eagerly.

CHAPTER 8
"I AM READY TO DIE!"

B ARON OSCAR ZU LAMBRECHT was an unhappy man. He paced up and down in the corridor outside the Emperor's suite in the Waldorf-Astoria, one of the few hotels that had survived the bombardment. It was late afternoon, and the Emperor was holding a reception of his officers. Gaily uniformed men were passing continuously, bowing respectfully to the baron. A steady stream of officers were making their way toward the reception room, where they would pay their respects to the Master of Europe and Asia, and of part of America. They all looked enviously at the Baron Oscar zu Lambrecht, attired so gorgeously in his colorful uniform of a marshal of the Empire.

But Oscar was not happy. There were little beads of perspiration on his round, bald dome, and there was sweat on the back on his hands. A passing dignitary saluted him, bowed respectfully, asked pleasantly: "How is it that Your Excellency is not at the side of His Imperial Majesty?" There was an almost imperceptible edge of sarcasm in the man's voice. "The Emperor has leaned so constantly upon your counsel of late, that it is surprising to see you not near him."

Oscar muttered something unintelligible, waited till the other had passed on, then squared his shoulders and headed for the reception room, like someone going to his execution.

The main ballroom of the hotel had been decorated for the occasion. It was a military reception, and there was a buffet along one side. At the far end was a dais upon which sat Maximilian I. The Emperor's short, squat body appeared almost ridiculous in his long purple robes. But one could easily imagine how he had ascended to the power he now possessed, by looking at his sharp, hawklike nose, his ruthless, cold eyes, and his thin, cruel mouth.

There were a few women present—the wives and relatives of many American citizens who had been compelled to attend. A hidden orchestra was playing, and several couples were dancing.

A bevy of officers opened a path for Baron Oscar zu Lambrecht as he approached the dais, almost reluctantly, and bowed low before the Emperor. Maximilian frowned at him. "Come closer, Oscar. There are some things I have to say to you!"

Oscar said: "Yes, sire," and stepped up on the dais, stood beside the Emperor. Maximilian waved the others back. Then he said fiercely to his satellite: "So! Oscar is a smart man, eh?

He baited a trap for Operator 5, did he not? And this Operator 5 slipped right into your trap, my fine fellow, and then slipped out again—taking the bait along with him!"

Oscar squirmed, but said nothing. The Emperor proceeded coldly: "You had everything arranged, didn't you? The square was thoroughly guarded, wasn't it? And yet you trusted the execution to such a pompous fool as Colonel Mainz—who could be fooled by a few firecrackers into taking all his men out of the square!"

The sweating baron raised his eyes from the floor, protested weakly: "But, sire, how could I know that Mainz would allow himself—?"

"Silence! It was your business to know. The successful man is he who knows how to choose competent subordinates. That is why my armies are victorious. That is why I have already conquered half the world—because I know how to choose my generals. I thought," he added, "that I knew how to choose my counselors as well. I see that I was mistaken. Oscar, you have failed—"

"But, sire, I have served you faithfully in so many other matters. After all, this business of Operator 5 is only a small matter—"

"A small matter? If you had been here, you would have heard the latest news. He has seized one of my gunboats, and with it, he has rescued the survivors of his band of guerrillas, whom we had bottled up at the powerhouse. He sailed out into the harbor with his men. Did you not hear cannonading a little while ago?"

"Yes, sire, I heard—"

"That was this precious Operator 5. He stole up on the fleet.

86

They suspected nothing, and he sank two ships of the line. They were entirely unprepared, and he blew them out of the water. A small matter, eh?"

Oscar's face was pale. "Your Majesty, if you will forgive me this time, I swear that I will capture this Operator 5—"

MAXIMILIAN WAVED him to silence. "That is not necessary. He is as good as captured. I shall give you another chance. If you fail now, though, there shall be no forgiveness. Here—read this! It was delivered by a boy, who left it with one of the guards and disappeared before he could be questioned."

Oscar took the sheet of paper, spread it open, and mumbled the contents to himself as he read:

> To His Imperial Majesty
> Maximilian I,
> Emperor of Europe and Asia,
>
> Greetings!
> Your ultimatum has been transmitted to me. I shall comply with your terms. In return for your promise to refrain from using the Green Gas upon my countrymen, I shall surrender myself to the Baron Oscar zu Lambrecht, Commandant of the New York area, punctually at sundown tonight. Since your ultimatum said nothing about how I was to occupy myself before sundown, I have taken the liberty of capturing one of your ships and of sinking two others. It's too bad that I can't be executed more than once, isn't it?
>
> Trusting that my execution will give you as much pleasure as it will cause me regret, I am

Operator 5.

The orchestra ceased playing, and the brilliantly uniformed officers bowed to their partners, applauded elegantly. But Oscar heard nothing. His eyes were glowing. "Then my idea to threaten them with the Green Gas was successful! Your Majesty will recall that it was my suggestion—"

"Yes, yes. I recall it, and that is why I am giving you another chance after your failure of this morning. But this time, Oscar, you must not fail! I suspect some trick on the part of this daredevil. I cannot believe that a man will voluntarily surrender himself to death without hoping in some way to save himself."

"Ah, sire," Oscar murmured, "you do not understand these Yankees. They are chivalrous to the point of idiocy. He is no doubt glad to sacrifice himself to save the million who might perish—"

Maximilian leered. "But if he knew that we are going to use to Green Gas anyway, tomorrow?"

Oscar gasped. "But, Majesty! It was your wish not to destroy the population of this country, so that after the conquest we could use its resources to conquer the rest of the Americas!"

"True, Oscar. But in spite of our superior armament, our advance has been too slow. Today, the Americans fought every inch of ground that they gave us, even though we laid down the severest barrage since we began the campaign. They have us stopped just outside of Washington now. We must take their capital tomorrow, and deliver such a blow that the rest of the country will hasten to yield. That is why I plan to use the Green Gas tomorrow. I have instructed General Klauber to release sufficient gas to flood the territory from Washington to the James River, and from the Chesapeake Bay westward to the section which these Yankees call the Shenandoah National Park. It is a territory of ninety square miles. It will destroy more than two million civilians, and perhaps a third as many troops. It will be a blow that will bring the whole nation to its knees!"

OSCAR SAID guardedly: "Does Your Majesty think it wise? These Yankees are strange. Instead of disheartening them, it may stir them up—"

"Let it!" Maximilian snapped. "We will use more! Now go, and prepare to receive this Operator 5. The sun will go down in an hour." His thin lips tightened. "Prepare an execution block here, within this hotel. I shall invite all my guests to witness Operator 5's death. And get another executioner to take the place of Willfred. Hurry! And see that nothing goes wrong this time!"

The baron was about to depart when an indolent, haughty voice at his elbow spoke:

"Oscar is a fool, Father. You should have him beheaded!"

New beads of sweat appeared on Oscar's round face. He turned, looked fearfully at the foppish young man who had appeared behind him. "Highness!" he muttered.

The young man's face was dissipated, cruel. The thin mouth and sharp nose were almost identical with those of Maximilian I. But the chin was receding, and there was a queer red glint in his eyes.

He was dressed carefully, gorgeously. A string of medals decorated his gold-embroidered tunic. Oscar had not noticed it, but a hush had descended upon the room when he had entered and walked up to the dais, nodding curtly here and there to those who bowed to him.

This was Crown Prince Rudolph, the son of Maximilian I. However cruel and relentless Maximilian was, it would be a sorry day for the Central Empire and for the rest of the world when Rudolph ascended the throne.

The Emperor glanced indulgently at his son. "What have you done with Colonel Mainz, Rudolph? Have you punished him for his negligence this morning?"

The Crown Prince laughed. His pointed teeth showed between red lips. "He is punished, Father. I took care of it myself. The fool begged for mercy. Ha, ha! Mercy! I was merciful—I beheaded him with my own hands. And he did not have the grace to thank me for the signal honor I did him!"

Oscar shuddered. "You—beheaded Mainz? He was a faithful officer, Highness. Perhaps he made a mistake—"

"Stop!" Rudolph's eyes glowed madly. "Do you question my acts?"

"No, no, Highness!" cried Oscar, recoiling a step. "Whatever Your Highness does—is altogether right."

Maximilian interrupted, impatiently. "Leave off, Rudolph. Oscar is still my minister. Do not heckle him. Go, Oscar. Make arrangements for Operator 5's execution!"

Rudolph said: "Is Operator 5 really coming to give himself up?"

Maximilian nodded.

"Father! I beg a favor of you!"

"What is it, Rudolph?"

"Let me wield the broadsword that severs his head. I love to slice heads off. I should have been born an executioner instead of a prince."

Maximilian shrugged. "Very well."

"Thank you, Father!" Rudolph, excited as much as if his father had just given him the world to play with, kissed Maximilian's hand, turned and left, smiling at everyone. He called back: "Have me notified when everything is ready, Oscar. I am going to select a sharp sword for this distinguished captive!"

WHEN HE had gone, the orchestra commenced playing again, and couples resumed their dancing. Maximilian said to Oscar: "I wish that my son were a little less—bloodthirsty. If I should ever die, Oscar," his eyes twinkled, "beware of losing your head!" He waved his hand. "You may go now."

The baron bowed low, backed off the dais. Maximilian watched him depart, then turned to the brilliantly gowned men and women who were waiting at a respectful distance. Among them were many of the wives and daughters of the officials of the Central Empire. Their husbands and fathers had brought them along across the ocean, because they did not know when they would return home. Maximilian had hinted that he might settle in the Americas with his court, and govern the world from here.

These people crowded around him at his smile now, uttering flattering remarks, complimenting him on the successes of the army during the day.

Suddenly, a breathless officer appeared in the doorway, made his way swiftly across the room to the dais. "Majesty!"

Crown Prince
Rudolph

he exclaimed, bowing. "Operator 5 has come. He has given himself up!"

Maximilian half-rose in his seat. His sharp eyes expressed triumph. "Good!" he said. "That is the best news I have heard today. Where is he?"

"He is outside, sire, under guard."

"Bring him in. We will talk to this Operator 5. He should

Emperor
Maximilian I

amuse us for a little time—while Oscar prepares for the execution!"

The officer retired, while the whisper ran around the crowded room that Operator 5 had arrived. Men and women cast curious glances toward the door, awaiting their first glimpse of the almost legendary figure of the man who had been a thorn in the side of the powerful Maximilian.

Measured footsteps sounded in the outer hall, and in a moment a detail of eight gray-uniformed soldiers appeared, in two columns, following their officer. Between the two columns marched the prisoner. A great gasp went up from the assembled company at sight of the big, broad-shouldered man who marched between the guards to his death.

Women murmured to their escorts: "He must be very brave—but he doesn't look very intelligent. Who would think that he was clever enough to have planned all those raids?"

Maximilian himself followed the prisoner's approach to the dais with gloating, cruel eyes.

The guard detail stopped at the foot of the Emperor's chair, and one of them prodded the prisoner forward. He stood straight and firm, staring Maximilian in the face. None of these people present had ever seen Operator 5. They did not know that Operator 5 was younger, slimmer, more alert of eye and bearing than this man.

They did not know that the man who stood a prisoner before the Emperor now was not Operator 5 at all, but a prizefighter, Plugger Dugan by name!

The Emperor said gloatingly: "So you are Operator 5? Are you ready to die?"

And Plugger Dugan, without hesitation, replied: "I am Operator 5. I am ready to die!"

CHAPTER 9
"LONG LIVE THE EMPEROR!"

PLUGGER DUGAN was deliberately sacrificing himself in the place of Jimmy Christopher. Back on the gunboat earlier that afternoon, they had been cooking up a conspiracy—Diane, Nan, Slips, Tim and Plugger. They had seen Jimmy Christopher write the note to Maximilian and send Tim Donovan ashore with it with instructions to leave it with a guard near the Imperial quarters, then to return to the Battery and await the boat which was to bring Operator 5 ashore that evening.

After Tim Donovan had gone, Jimmy Christopher entered the cabin where they were sitting and cooking up their scheme. Jimmy looked around from one to the other of them, and the grimness he had worn for the last few hours disappeared. Nan and Diane came up to him, and he put an arm around each, hugged them. "I'm sorry I was short-tempered with you all before," he said. "I know that you wanted to keep me from giving myself up."

Nan exclaimed: "We don't want you to die, Jimmy. If I wanted to keep the message from you, it's because—we all love you—"

"But how about the men and women and children who would die tonight if the Green Gas were released? They also have people who love them." He shook his head. "No, I've got to go."

Diane broke in. "You're too valuable, Jimmy. Look at the things you've done behind the lines here. And if you leave us, who'll manage this ship? We're wandering around, with planes out looking for us, with battleships steaming around in search of us—"

"You can sail around to Newport News," Jimmy told her. "There are several men on board who know how to navigate. If you leave tonight, you'll get to Newport News before our Defense Force is driven back. You can join Dad at headquarters—"

Slips McGuire interrupted hastily: "But look, Boss—how do you know that this here Maximilian won't use the Green Gas tomorrow? By giving yourself up you ain't stopping him from using it."

"I've got to take that chance, Slips. As it stands now, he'll surely use it tonight if I don't surrender."

"Then you're determined to go?" Diane asked him, low-voiced. He nodded. "It's in the books, Di."

Diane turned away from him, her shoulders drooping. Nan sighed.

Jimmy said flatly: "Well, I might as well start now." He went over to Diane, took both her hands. "You understand, Di?"

She blinked her eyes to keep back the tears, forced a smile. "I—understand, Jimmy."

Slowly he took her in his arms, and she clung to him, her wet face close to his.

The others turned their backs. Plugger Dugan whispered to Nan: "What about my idea, Miss Christopher? I'd be glad to go instead o' him."

Nan shook her head. "It's—fine of you, Plugger. But—you mustn't."

JIMMY HAD left Diane. He kissed Nan, shook hands with Slips and with Plugger, started out of the cabin. "I'll go with you, Cap," Dugan said suddenly. "There's something I want to talk to you about before you go."

He went out into the companionway with Jimmy. Jimmy said: "What is it, Plugger?"

"Come in here a minute, Cap. This cabin is empty, an' we can talk in here."

Jimmy followed him into the vacant cabin. "Make it snappy, Plugger. I haven't got much time."

"Sure, Cap, sure. I'll make it snappy. Look—" he was standing in front of Operator 5, and he brought up his huge fist, bunched, in a terrific right uppercut to the point of Jimmy's jaw. Operator 5 wasn't expecting anything like that. His head snapped back, his eyes glazed, and he sank slowly to the floor, fighting ineffectually against the blackness that engulfed him.

Plugger Dugan lifted him tenderly, placed him on the cot. He said softly: "I hope you won't be sore at me when you wake up, Operator 5. You're a grand guy—too damn grand to get rubbed out right now. Me, I'm nobody—just a guy with muscle and no brains. Nobody'll miss me."

Working swiftly, he changed tunics with Jimmy. The tunic of the staff officer, which Jimmy had worn, was a little tight for Plugger, but he now wore the same clothing in which it was known that Operator 5 had disguised himself. They might not know Jimmy's face, but they would know the uniform. He fingered the two long, colored tubes that he found in the lining of Jimmy's coat. He knew what they were—tubes of concentrated explosive, far more powerful than Mills bombs. He stared at them a second, then put them grimly into his pocket.

Jimmy was breathing slowly, stertorously. Plugger nodded. If there was one thing he knew how to do, it was how to knock a man out. He extracted the key from the inside of the lock, stepped outside, peered furtively up and down the companion-way, and locked the door, then hurried forward.

A boat had been lowered and was waiting, with a crew. They were to run Jimmy ashore, pick up Tim Donovan, and come back.

The man in charge of the boat crew, Harry Gillett, looked at Dugan questioningly. Plugger said, "I'm goin' instead o' Operator 5, Harry."

Gillett said: "He let you go?" He was a bit incredulous.

Dugan winked. "The chief has figgered out a stunt to put it over on Maximilian. That's why I'm goin'. Let's get started."

Gillett shrugged, and they got into the boat, pulled away. Dugan looked back, saw that Diane and Nan had come up on deck, and were waving good-by. Plugger grinned. They couldn't tell, at this distance, that he wasn't Operator 5. Everything was going off smoothly so far....

WHEN PLUGGER DUGAN stood before Maximilian and said: "I am ready to die," he meant it. Dugan had fought his way up to the heavyweight championship by the power of his punches, and the ability to "take it". He had never given much thought to questions of idealism or patriotism. All he knew was how to stand up and dish it out in a square ring. He put his money away, and he had become quite wealthy, as champions

The bomb exploded in a blinding holocaust!

do nowadays. No thought of the future had ever bothered him, nor had any questions entered his skull as to the welfare of the human race.

But when he saw his country invaded, saw men and women slaughtered, saw people forced to labor for the conqueror, something had surged up within him that had made him speak up that morning at the public library. And he had seen how a man may devote himself to the cause of others—he had watched Jimmy Christopher, had seen the reckless courage with which Operator 5 risked everything for the sake of his country. And Plugger Dugan became a different man.

Admiration for Jimmy Christopher had caused him to do the thing he was doing now—admiration and a sudden sort of doglike devotion. He was like a man inspired. Maximilian looked at him queerly. "You are a brave man!" he said softly. "You know that you are going to be beheaded?"

"I know it. As long as you don't use that Green Gas—"

"I am afraid, my friend, that I must disappoint you. My envoy to your general made no promises. He only said that if you did not give yourself up by sundown, we would spread the gas. He did not say that we would promise not to use it if you did give yourself up. Do you see the distinction?"

Plugger looked at the Emperor dully. "You mean—you're going to use the Green Gas—anyway?"

Maximilian frowned. "You are a little dull, my friend—for one who is reputed to be so clever. It took you quite a while to get my meaning."

"You're going to kill a million people with that gas that bloats them up and turns them purple?"

"I am, my friend. But it should be some consolation to you, that you will not be able to witness the agony of your country-men. The eyes of a severed head cannot see."

Plugger Dugan's face grew red. "Damn you!" he shouted, "you won't see it either!" And his hand dove in under his tunic, came out with one of the little fountain-pen bombs he had taken from Jimmy Christopher. He put the pin of the bomb in his teeth, pulled at it.

Someone shouted: "A bomb!"

Maximilian clutched the arms of his chair, screamed: "Stop him!"

The guards had backed away from the dais while the pris-oner talked to the Emperor. Now they rushed in at Plugger, but Dugan had the pin out, was raising his arm to hurl the bomb. Two soldiers leaped upon him, but he sent them reeling with two backhand blows. Then he sprang backward. The other soldiers leveled rifles, poured lead into Dugan's body. The sharp explosions of the guns mingled with the screams of women and the enraged shouts of officers.

Slug after slug crashed into the huge form of Plugger Dugan, but he kept on his feet, laughing. "I can take it!" he shouted and hurled the bomb. He had waited just the right length of time. The bomb exploded in a blinding holocaust of light and thun-der just as it hit the dais. Maximilian vanished in a cloud of smoke and fire!

Plugger Dugan stood there, wavering on his feet, full of lead, blood spurting from a dozen wounds, while flames leaped up from the spot where Maximilian had been. Men in uniform rushed at the big, bleeding man. More and more bullets lodged in his body. And he still laughed.

At last he sank to the floor, laughing. And he died with that triumphant laugh on his lips....

THE FIRE spread immediately, ravenously. Men and women turned to run from the room, the soldiers going with them, leaving within the body of their dead Emperor and the riddled body of the man who had killed him. Plugger Dugan, who had perished gladly, with a laugh on his lips, had done more in a moment than the armies of America had done in twenty-two days—he had deprived the Central Empire of its Emperor.

Plugger Dugan, prizefighter, shared the funeral pyre with Maximilian I, Emperor of Europe and Asia.

Outside, the brilliantly uniformed officers and the gaily dressed women gathered in a crowd to watch the flames lick from the huge Waldorf-Astoria Building. The sun, a red ball in the west, rivaled the burning building with its brilliance. But they paid no attention to the sun. Panic spread through the throng. "The Emperor is dead!" went up the cry. "The Emperor is dead! Operator 5 has killed the Emperor!"

Men kept pouring from the burning hotel. The bomb contained chemicals which, in addition to causing the explosion, aided the fire to spread. The hotel was doomed.

Suddenly, all eyes turned to the brightly uniformed figure who came dashing out of the building, wild-eyed, trembling. It was Rudolph, the Crown Prince. He had had a narrow escape, for the flames were lapping at his heels. A couple of officers supported him on their arms.

The shouts of the crowd suddenly changed from "The Emperor is dead!" to "Long live the Emperor!"

Rudolph looked up at the new cry and it took him a moment to realize what they meant. Suddenly his chest went out, and he stood erect. All thought of his father, dead on the dais, fled from him. He raised a hand in a salute to the throng. And the cry redoubled: "Long live the Emperor!"

Rudolph I, cruel, far more merciless than his father, now was Emperor of the Central Empire. He smiled madly, said to the two officers who were supporting him: "*Now* we will show these Yankees what a reign of terror is like! And we'll begin with a little terror right at home. Where is Oscar?"

The two officers shuddered at the stark hate in Rudolph's voice. They had known that the Crown Prince disliked his father's minister, but they had never suspected that he hated the man with such intensity. "We will look for him, sire," they said.

And far at the fringe of the crowd, Oscar, Baron zu Lambrecht, Marshal of the Empire, and Commandant of the Occupied Territory of New York, slunk away toward the river, shivering lest he be caught and delivered to the horrible mercies of the new Emperor....

CHAPTER 10
WALKING GHOST

N AN CHRISTOPHER said wearily: "I can't raise
G.H.Q., Jimmy. I've tried the private code, and the War
Department Edition, but I can't get a rumble!"

Operator 5 was pacing the bridge of the commandeered
gunboat. Diane Elliot was in the infirmary, tending a number
of the men who had minor wounds from the engagement at
the powerhouse. Tim Donovan was wandering around the ship,
checking on her stores and supplies. Slips McGuire, who had
revealed unexpected culinary prowess, had taken charge of the
galley, and was ordering around a couple of men who volun-
teered as assistant cooks.

Jimmy turned dully to Nan. He had a slight bruise on the left
side of his jaw. He had been staring moodily out to sea while the
gunboat steamed south along the coast. He said to Nan: "Did
you try a general call?"

She nodded. "There doesn't seem to be anything on the air.
It's as if the whole world was dead. Jimmy—I'm afraid!"

Operator 5 sighed. He closed his eyes hard, and opened them.
"It's twenty-five hours and fourteen minutes since sundown last
night. Plugger Dugan went to take the medicine that was being
brewed for me, just twenty-five hours and fourteen minutes ago.
He must be dead by this time. God! I can't stop thinking of it—
how he knocked me out so he could die in my place!"

Nan said huskily: "Jimmy, you believe me, don't you? You
believe I didn't approve what he planned?"

104

"Of course, Nan. Of course I believe you."

"He told us all—Diane and Tim and Slips and me—about the idea. But we all vetoed it. We wouldn't let him do it. Much as we love you, Jimmy, we weren't going to let him die in your place. You never would have forgiven us. And then, in the cabin, when you told us your mind was made up to go, he whispered to me, and asked if he should do what he had suggested. I told him no. I never suspected, when he went out with you, that he would do anything like that."

Jimmy Christopher put a hand on his sister's shoulder. "It's over, Nan. Plugger Dugan was a brave man. I only hope that he didn't die in vain."

"What do you mean?"

Jimmy smiled bitterly. "Hasn't it occurred to you that there is nothing to prevent Maximilian from releasing the Green Gas, even though I've surrendered, as he thinks? He's equal to it. And then, I'm afraid Plugger may have done something desperate. There were two fountain pen bombs in the lining of my uniform tunic. I remember showing them to him, explaining how they worked. I thought he ought to know, since he'd become one of us. He may try to blow up the Emperor. If he tried, and failed, there may be retaliations. The silence on the air—"

Nan went and leaned against the rail, put her head in her hands. "The suspense is the worst part of it. Here we are, at sea, with no news, with no knowledge of what's been taking place in the last twenty-four hours." She swung around. "Where are we, anyway, Jimmy?"

He frowned. "We should be near Norfolk. But I can't see any

lights. You know how bright and gay Norfolk looks from the sea at night. I've kept the ship close into shore purposely—"

He stopped as a flare suddenly illumined the night close by, to the west, in the direction where land should be. At the same time the lookout called: "Land, ho!"

Jimmy picked up his night glasses, while the improvised crew of landsmen down on the deck below craned their necks toward the flare. Jimmy swept the stretch of sea between their ship and land, and he swore softly to himself. Nan behind him, asked: "What is it, Jimmy?"

NOW, AS additional flares went up, specks became visible on the sea. They came closer, resolved themselves into the shapes of small boats, launches, cabin boats, even some rowboats. There were thirty, forty, fifty of them, dotting the sea now. They were waving shirts, handkerchiefs, flags.

Jimmy moved the engine-room indicator to "slow," and then to "stop." The boats came closer, and Nan exclaimed: "Look! There are mostly women and children in them—and only a few men to run them! They—*Jimmy! They're fleeing from the land!*"

Operator 5 nodded grimly, watched the boats draw near. Suddenly, the leading boats slowed up, stopped, and veered around, began pulling away from them. "They're afraid of us!" Nan exclaimed.

"Sure they are! Look at that. We never took it down!" He pointed up at the white flag on the ship, with the black insignia of the crossed broadswords and the severed head. "We're still flying the emblem of the Central Empire!" He cupped his hands, shouted: "Haul down that flag!"

His order was obeyed with alacrity. They had flown the Central Empire flag at first because they were liable at any time to run into a squadron of enemy ships. And later Jimmy had had too much on his mind to remember it.

Now the gruesome emblem came down, and one of the men called up: "What'll we put up instead? We haven't got an American flag!"

Jimmy frowned, and just at that moment Diane appeared on deck, carrying something bundled up in her arms.

"Here's what you want," she announced. She shook out the thing she was carrying, held it up. It was the stars and stripes. The men on deck raised a shout. One of them took the flag from her, and soon it was billowing in the breeze—not a naval pennant, but a good old-fashioned flag.

A cheer went up from the men, and the boats out at sea seemed to halt in their flight. The crew stood at the rail, waving and shouting, and after a moment the boats began to approach slowly.

Diane came up on the bridge, and Nan said: "Di! Where did you get the flag?"

"I made it," said Diane, simply. "I knew we had no flag, and I sewed it while I was in the infirmary. The men got me old sweaters, neckties and sheets. It's makeshift, but it ought to let the world know who we are!" She looked up proudly at her handiwork.

Jimmy Christopher grinned. He saluted Diane. "Miss Betsy Ross the Second!" he said. "That's what this country needs instead of a five-cent cigar! It needs more of the spirit that we had 1776! If there were a hundred million more like you, Di, the Central Empire army would have to swim home!"

By this time the boats had drawn closer, within hailing distance. They still appeared doubtful of their welcome, thinking perhaps that the hoisting of the American flag was some sort of ruse. A feeble hail came from the nearest boat: "What ship is that?"

Jimmy used the megaphone: "This is a United States gunboat now. What's your trouble?"

There was silence for a moment, then: "You sound like an American. But she looks like an enemy ship."

Jimmy chuckled: "It used to be an enemy ship. We've got it now. But never mind that. What are you doing out here in those boats?"

"We're refugees. The enemy is flooding the whole section with Green Gas. Thousands have died. If we stay on land we're lost!"

Jimmy exclaimed: "Good God!" He looked at Diane and Nan. "Maximilian did it anyway!" He shouted to the boats. "Come alongside. We'll take you on board."

THE BUSINESS of getting the refugees aboard the ship occupied more than three hours. It was tricky work. Though the sea was smooth enough, most of the women were excited, hysterical. In the cabin Jimmy received the leader of the refugees, a man of about fifty who was mayor of Norfolk, John Sommers by name.

Diane, Nan, Tim and Slips were busy ministering to the needs of the starved, frightened, spray-wet refugees. Sommers gulped the shot of rye that Jimmy gave him, wiped his mouth with a trembling hand. His face was drawn, his gray hair matted, his eyes reflecting the terrors of the last day and night.

"It was dreadful!" he said in a hushed voice. "Yesterday, at about seven o'clock, we got the first word that the Green Gas was being used at the front. It's heavy stuff, and it settles close to the ground. You can see it roll like waves. And wherever it touches, men crumble, and lie bloated and quivering. They turn blue and die." He shuddered. "We didn't think it would reach us, way down here. But it did. The Defense Force was destroyed—there's hardly a man survived out of the troops under General Humphrey's command. At the first news, they started evacuating Washington. The President and the Cabinet, and the War Department moved to Richmond. But G.H.Q. was destroyed."

Jimmy gripped Sommers' sleeve. "Everybody was killed at G.H.Q.?" He was thinking of his father. John Christopher had been there.

Sommers took another drink from the bottle on the table. "We couldn't get any news from Humphrey's headquarters. They must have been caught in the first wave of the gas. You know, Humphrey tried to set an example, by setting up his headquarters as close to the front as he could. After the gas got started, it spread fast. The first thing we knew, people were streaming into Norfolk and Portsmouth by the hundreds. They told of seeing others die as they fled. The gas hasn't hit Norfolk yet, because of the wind from the ocean. The wind turned it back. But as soon as the wind dies down, Norfolk will be flooded with it. Thousands of people left this morning in all the available ships. They headed south. I stayed to the last, with these people that you've just taken aboard."

Jimmy's lips pursed tightly. "At that rate, Maximilian could wipe out the whole country in a week!"

"And there's nothing we can do," Sommers said bitterly, "except capitulate. It's madness—fighting against a ruthless force like that. We've got to send a delegation to Rudolph—ask him on what terms he will accept the country's surrender—"

"Rudolph?" Jimmy asked, puzzled. "You mean Maximilian."

Sommers shook his head. "You haven't heard the latest news. I don't know who you are, but you must have been out of touch since you captured this ship. Maximilian was killed yesterday—assassinated. His son, Rudolph, the Crown Prince, is now ruler of the Central Empire. They dropped circulars from planes over our lines, announcing it. Here—" he pulled a wet, soggy sheet of paper from his pocket, handed it to Jimmy—"read it for yourself."

The proclamation was printed in two languages: that of the Central Empire, and that of the United States. It read:

PROCLAMATION!

Today, His Imperial Majesty, Maximilian I, Emperor of Europe and Asia, was assassinated by the cowardly guerrilla, Operator 5, who was killed as he completed his attempt.

Americans, prepare to pay the price of this dastardly crime!

We, Rudolph I, duly crowned Emperor of Europe and Asia, Lord of the Central Empire, promise that our father shall be avenged. Our vengeance shall reach through the length and the breadth of your country. Prepare for death, Americans!"

It was signed by the Emperor, Rudolph.

JIMMY CHRISTOPHER'S eyes burned as he read that document. "So that's why they're flooding the country with gas. This Rudolph mast be a devil!"

Sommers nodded. "That's why we must beg for peace at any price. He holds it in his power to wipe out every bit of life from coast to coast. This Operator 5 did us no favor when he assassinated Maximilian. The fool! Didn't he know that something like this would follow? It's a good thing for him that he was killed. Or else he could lie awake nights, and think of the millions of bloated, purple men and women and children lying in hideous death everywhere, as the result of his act of folly!"

Jimmy Christopher faced him, his face a mask. He hadn't told any of these people, yet, who he was. The others had been too happy to be rescued to ask any questions, and Sommers had been too full of information to be curious. Now, Jimmy said to the older man: "What if this Operator 5 did not die? What if he were still alive?"

Sommers' eyes blazed. "Then he ought to be caught and strung up by the neck! He ought to be made to pay for the death and destruction he has brought upon us!"

"Perhaps it wasn't Operator 5 who did it."

"No, no, it was he. Maximilian wanted his head. He threatened to use the Green Gas against us if Operator 5 didn't give himself up. Well, this Operator 5 did give himself up. And he tried to make himself a national hero, a martyr, by killing Maximilian, not giving a thought to the fact that the Central Empire forces still controlled the Green Gas. Of course they would take steps to avenge their Emperor. No, my friend, this Operator 5 has done us more harm than any traitor could ever have done. If he's alive, he should be hanged. Before leaving Washington, the President issued an order striking the name of Operator 5 from the rolls of the United States Intelligence. He will not even be reported as having died in the performance of his duty. His name shall forever be anathema to citizens of this country!"

Jimmy Christopher lowered his eyes before Sommers' gaze. He started, as he became conscious of a figure in the doorway. He turned, saw his sister, Nan, standing there. She had heard everything, and her blazing eyes, her clenched fists as she gazed at the elderly mayor of Norfolk, told of the anger within her. She took a single step toward Sommers. Whatever she might have said, however, Jimmy stopped. "Nan!" he called sharply. She glanced at him, and he shook his head.

Nan subsided....

"And now, Mr. Sommers," Jimmy said, "if you will excuse me, I have some matters to attend to. We are steaming due south, and will set you and your companions down at some spot where the gas has not reached. Your quarters will be assigned to you. I hope you will he comfortable."

When Sommers had left, Nan swung on Operator 5. "Jimmy! Why did you let him say such things about you? Why didn't you tell him the truth—that you weren't even there—that you had nothing to do with Maximilian's death?"

"Because," Jimmy said somberly, "I wouldn't have been believed. No one would believe that I had been knocked out by a man who deliberately did it to take my place, in order to die. Men don't believe that other men are capable of such sacrifice. And in the second place, even if they did believe it, I am not going to sully the name of Plugger Dugan. He was very brave, and he was very devoted to me. I am alive now because of what he did. Shall I repay him by betraying his name?"

Nan flung away from him in a dudgeon. "You're a fool, Jimmy—a sentimental fool. You always were. People think you're a strong, silent man. Well, I'm your sister, and I know different. What does Dugan care, now, what is said about him? I'm sure he'd want you to tell the truth and clear your own name." She sighed. "But I know you won't do it—and—" she threw her arms around his neck, hugged him tight—"I love you for being like that, Jimmy!"

HE SMILED suddenly, pressed her close. "Thanks, Nan. I knew you'd understand."

As a matter of fact, it was very easy for Nan to understand her twin brother. As they stood there in the cabin, there was an ethereal resemblance between them, in addition to the physical. Nan was something like a more delicate replica of Jimmy—like an oil painting that has been reproduced in watercolor by another artist who, perhaps, has a lighter touch.

Nan was quick to sense her brother's moods. And now she said suddenly: "Jimmy! You're keeping something from me! There's something you're—afraid to tell me!"

He lowered his eyes. "No, no, Nan. It's nothing definite—"

"It is, Jimmy, it is! You can't fool me." Her voice was curiously strained, husky. "Tell me, Jimmy. Is it—Dad?"

113

He nodded, mutely, and she gasped. "He's—?"

"I don't know, Nan. He was at G.H.Q., and the whole district was flooded with the Green Gas. Sommers doesn't know for sure, but he thinks G.H.Q. was swamped by the gas."

It was characteristic of Nan that she did not burst into tears, did not sob, did not become hysterical. She merely stood there, and closed her eyes, her little fists clenched at her sides, and her young breasts heaving with repressed emotion. Then she opened her eyes, and looked long into her brother's. A shudder went through her slim body. "Dad!" she said brokenly. "Good, brave Dad—" her voice was pitched low—"he would have wanted to die a clean death, on his feet, fighting. Instead—to be swollen and bloated and blue—"

"Stop, Nan!" Jimmy cried, and reached out and gripped her arm. His fingers dug into her soft flesh. "Stop! We mustn't think. There's too much to do. And maybe—it's not so." He looked away, saw Diane Elliot at the door. She was gazing at them both with eyes that were full of sympathy. She had not heard what they said, but she knew at once that some great sorrow was clawing at their hearts.

Jimmy said to her: "Di, take Nan away. I'll see you both later. There's something I've got to attend to."

Nan said nothing. She pressed Jimmy's hand, went to the door stiffly, blinking her eyes. They were moist at the corners. Diane said: "Dear!" and put her arms around her. "It must be something dreadful. Come and tell me about it."

The two girls were leaving when Jimmy called after them: "And by the way—will you do something for me, Di?"

"Of course."

"Get Tim and Slips. Let them circulate among our boys, and whisper to them that they're not to mention who I am. The refugees must not know that Operator 5 is on this ship. They think me dead. Let them go on thinking that way."

Diane didn't ask why. She nodded. "I'll tell them, Jimmy."

After they were gone, Jimmy sat moodily for a while, his eyes roving about the cabin, resting on the huge broadsword of Willfred's, which had been stood up in the corner with the point resting against the floor, the broad, black hilt leaning against the wall.

He pressed the button which buzzed out on the bridge, and when one of his officers entered in response, he said: "Luke, go and get that executioner, Willfred, out of the closet where he's been locked, and bring him here. I want to talk to him."

IN A few minutes, the surly Willfred entered, guarded by Luke and another man. Jimmy waved them out. "You can leave us alone. I want to talk to him in private."

When they were alone, Jimmy got up and faced the executioner. Willfred was still naked to the waist, as he had been in New York. He was looking at Jimmy half-fearfully.

Jimmy said: "Willfred, you are now a prisoner of the Americans. You are the man who has cut off many American heads. When I turn you over to the authorities, you can imagine what to expect?"

He spoke in the native language of the executioner, and Willfred's eyes showed that he knew only too well what to expect.

He opened his mouth, ran his tongue around his thick lips. "The Americans—" he asked—"they do not behead?"

"No. But they have what is called the electric chair. They strap you into it, and attach wires to you. Then they pull a switch, and many thousand volts of electric current race through your body. Do you know how that feels?"

Willfred's nose twitched, his lips moved spasmodically. "One burns up? It must be frightful."

"You will know soon enough."

"They will do that to me?"

"Unless I decide not to turn you over to them."

"You—would save me from that chair that burns?"

"I might—if you were to tell me something I want to know."

"I will tell you anything—rather than burn!"

"All right. Then we understand each other. If you don't know the answers to the questions I am going to ask you, that will be too bad—for on the other hand, if you know the answers, there is a powerboat riding alongside this ship. We are not far from shore. You can go aboard it, and leave us—a free man!"

"Ask me."

"I want to know about the Green Gas. Where do they keep it? How do they make it?"

"I know nothing of that." Willfred's glance had suddenly become cunning, at mention of the powerboat. His eyes flicked to the big sword in the corner, then to Jimmy, noting that he wore no revolver. Plugger Dugan had neglected to leave his revolver when he changed tunics with Jimmy, and Operator 5 hadn't bothered to supply himself with another while they were aboard ship. "I know nothing of that," Willfred repeated.

"That is too bad—for you," Jimmy said softly.

Willfred's eyes were gleaming madly. "Too bad? Not for me. For you."

And he leaped across the room, seized the huge broadsword in his two powerful hands, raised it high above his head, and leaped at Jimmy.

Jimmy sidestepped nimbly, and the sword *swished* past his shoulder with a nasty sound. Had it struck him it would have sliced his arm off.

Willfred was thrown off balance by the blow, but he was used to his sword, and he recovered amazingly, wielding the weapon as if it had been a toy. His powerful shoulder and arm muscles rippled as he handled it. He raised it once more, snarling. Jimmy backed against the wall. The cot was on one side, the table on the other. He could not dodge the next blow. He was apparently defenseless.

Willfred bared his teeth. "There is much noise outside. No one would hear you if you were to shout. I thank you for telling me about the powerboat. I shall kill you, and be in it and away before those fools outside know what is happening!"

He swung the sword in a terrific blow at Jimmy's head.

Jimmy Christopher's hand had moved to the buckle of his belt, under the tunic, while Willfred spoke. Now, suddenly, his hand flashed away from the belt. He had released the buckle, and the belt seemed to spring away from his body like a live thing, and to straighten out in his hand. A flick of that hand, and the

117

leather sheath fell away from the long, flashing rapier of glinting Toledo steel which had nestled inside the belt.

THE WHOLE thing had taken but the fraction of an instant, while Willfred's ungainly sword was descending in that awkward blow to Jimmy's head. Now, the rapier flashed up before Willfred's eyes, and engaged the big broadsword, slithering along the wide blade. The broadsword slipped away from its course, fell wide of the mark.

Willfred, eyes popping from his head, fell back a step, while Jimmy Christopher's supple wrist sent the rapier whirling in dazzling, flashing circles in front of him.

The executioner snarled, swung his sword again in a powerful, dangerous slicing blow. And once more the supple rapier deflected the bigger weapon. Jimmy stepped in, lips tight and grim, lunged, and the point of the rapier passed under Willfred's sword, entered the executioner's side high up under the right arm. Willfred uttered a shriek; the sword fell from his useless hand as blood spurted out of the wound in a geyserlike stream.

For a moment the executioner looked down stupidly at the blood spouting from his body. It must have been strange to him to see his own blood spurting that way, after having witnessed the flowing blood of so many others whom he had beheaded. He stood there, swaying, raised frightened eyes to Jimmy, and then slowly buckled and fell to the floor, groaning, whimpering, one hand pressed hard to his side as if that would stem the carmine flow.

He mumbled: "I die. A doctor! A doctor!"

Jimmy first stepped around him, and pressed the buzzer. Then he knelt beside the executioner, without touching him, and said: "You are badly wounded. But it is a wound that a doctor can heal—I was careful about that. Now, I give you your last chance. Tell me about the Green Gas, and I will summon a doctor for you. Otherwise, I will leave you here to die!"

Willfred's face was gray with pain and terror. He, who had laughed at sight of so many rolling heads, was craven when death tapped him on the shoulder.

"Yes, yes—oh, God, the pain—I will speak! The Green Gas—I do not know how they make it. There is a formula. Only three men know where it is kept. They are the Emperor, his son, the Crown Prince Rudolph, and Baron Oscar—" he writhed in agony for a moment, but Jimmy did not put out a hand to touch him—"zu Lambrecht. Each time they need a supply of gas, they bring in five students of chemistry. They take out the formula and give it to these five, and the five work two days and two nights. They make the gas—and then—the five fools—are beheaded. Thus, there is no man—living—who knows—the formula."

Willfred let his head drop to the floor. He was gasping with pain. "I have spoken the truth. Get me a doctor. Stop this bleeding. I do—not wish—to die!"

Jimmy felt his whole body tingling with the excitement of the moment. Here was the first definite step toward discovering the secret of the Green Gas. He felt that Willfred had told the truth. There was still a long row to hoe before arriving at the goal— many dangers to be surmounted. But the road was indicated. He arose, his eyes shining, as Luke entered in answer to his ring.

"Take this man down to the infirmary," he ordered. "Have him treated. His wound isn't serious at all. I pinked him through the ribs. He thought he was dying!"

Luke stared, amazed, at the rapier still in Jimmy's hand, dripping blood, and at the broadsword on the floor. "Y-yes, sir!" he stammered.

Jimmy found the sheath, belted his rapier again, and went out in search of Diane and Nan. He found them in one of the cabins, with Tim and Slips McGuire.

Nan had a hold on herself, though her eyes were red, and her lower lip flecked with blood where she had bitten it. Jimmy made no reference to the fight in the other cabin. He asked: "Did you tell the boys not to say anything to the refugees about who I am?"

Tim and Slips nodded. Tim Donovan said: "We told everybody. Mum's the word. But why, Jimmy?"

"I'll tell you," Jimmy Christopher said. "They think I'm dead, up there in New York. So do our own people. I'm going back as soon as we land—somehow. And I want them all to keep on thinking I'm dead. From now on, Operator 5 is a ghost!"

Diane, sitting on the cot with an arm around Nan, looked up at Jimmy and shuddered at the grim expression on his face. "A—walking ghost!" she said, very low.

CHAPTER 11
TRAITOR'S TREATY

N IGHT LAY over the city of Jacksonville, Florida, like a black pall of terror. Men walked the streets fearfully, always glancing toward the north, as if expecting some dread specter of doom to descend upon them from that direction.

In the square before the courthouse, companies of armed men paraded by, while drummers and buglers played halfheartedly. These men were not regular army; neither were they national guard. They had rifles, and they tried to march with military snap and vigor. But they didn't keep their lines straight, and they didn't all carry their rifles at the proper angle on their shoulders. They were men from all walks of life, recruited hurriedly to form a Second Defense Army—to take the place of the divisions that had been destroyed at the Front by the Green Gas. They wore no uniforms, for uniforms were not available. Their rifles were not of the latest type, but were arms salvaged from old stores.

Their officers were little more seasoned than the impromptu troops—with here and there a sprinkling of regular army men.

Throughout the country tonight, these minute men of a modern day were flocking to the defense of their tortured country. And with them, in many cases, marched women. This new Green Gas represented a violently different type of warfare from any they had ever known—even those who were veterans of the World War. For it spread quickly, acted intensively, and destroyed by the hundred of thousand.

Yet these men marched to fight an enemy whom they could not hope to touch except by a miracle!

On the outside of the Jacksonville Courthouse, before which these men marched, was a small sign. It read:

TEMPORARY HEADQUARTERS
The President of the United States of America

On the steps stood a harrowed man, whose face was lined with the terror of the things that had happened to the country to which he was the Chief Executive.

Automatically he raised his hand in salute each time an improvised standard passed him. The beat of the drums and shrill of the bugles sent a separate pang through his heart each time they sounded.

He was reviewing the last resources of the United States. And he knew as he gazed at those brave, patriotic men and women who marched in review before him, that tomorrow they might be nothing but bloated, rotting corpses, decimated by the Green Gas of his country's ruthless conqueror.

He turned to a uniformed, hard-faced man in the uniform of a Brigadier-General, who stood at his right. "General Redfern, I am entrusting these brave people to your command. You are to carry on the work of General Humphrey. And I hope to God that you may not meet the same fate that he did!"

General Redfern nodded gloomily. "I shall do my best, sir. If we die, then perhaps it will be better. We will not live to see the country we love licking the boots of a dictator!" He glanced venomously at a black-haired, black-eyed man with a square jaw and thin lips who stood at the President's left. "If it hadn't been for Z-7's pet agent, Operator 5, we shouldn't be reduced to this dreadful state today. Rudolph would never have used the Green Gas, if Operator 5 hadn't killed his father!"

The man whom he referred to as Z-7 glared at General Redfern. His eyes burned into the other as he said: "Redfern, if you had one-tenth of the courage and the resource that Operator 5 had, you would understand that there must be something radically wrong about the report of his actions. How can you tell what prompted him to kill Maximilian? Perhaps it was to avert a still greater calamity that might have befallen us. I have always stood behind Operator 5, and in death I'll stand behind him, too. I resent your words, sir. You would never have had the courage to say them to the face of Operator 5—were he alive!"

REDFERN REDDENED, and his hand went to the automatic holstered at his belt. But the President, standing between the two men, said sharply: "Gentlemen! You forget where you are. Leave off this bickering. I have struck Operator 5's name from the rolls of the Intelligence. That is the worst thing we can do to a dead man. Let us say no more about it!"

Z-7 lowered his eyes. "I'm sorry, Mr. President. In times like these, one forgets oneself."

Just then, a uniformed messenger on a spitting motorcycle raced into the square from the direction of the river, and dismounted before the courthouse steps. He saluted General Redfern, and reported:

"The ship that we sighted a little while ago has docked at the foot of Duval Street, sir. It contains a number of refugees from

Norfolk. It is a Central Empire gunboat, but it was captured by a group of men in New York. Their leader is coming here now, to confer with you, sir. He will be here in a few moments."

Redfern grunted. "Must be a good man to have captured a gunboat. Who is he?"

"He refused to give his name, sir."

"Hmmph!" The general glanced at the President. "Sounds suspicious. Perhaps you'd better not see him—"

"Not see him? Of course I will. A man who has accomplished a feat like that—" The Chief Executive stopped, thoughtfully. "It reminds me of the kind of thing Operator 5 used to do. I'm sorry now that I struck his name from the rolls of the Intelligence. But I had to yield to the demands of public indignation. The people blame him for this gas attack."

The last of the marching men had left the square. Redfern saluted sternly. "Good-by, Mr. President. Depend upon me to do my best to hold the enemy in check. But with these ragged soldiers, and with the threat of the Green Gas—"

The President smiled. "I know you'll do your best, Redfern. I wish that I could go with you." He shook hands with the pompous general, watched him get stiffly into a staff car and drive away. The pitiful forces were going out to meet almost certain death. Redfern was pompous, egotistical. But he was a good general, and a brave man.

The President sighed, said to Z-7: "We'll go in now, and prepare to receive the miracle man who seized an enemy gunboat!"

The temporary office of the Chief Executive was in the courtroom on the main floor of the building. The President's desk was the old judge's bench. The rows of chairs had been removed, and the desks of his secretaries had been placed there. Gone was the traditional privacy of the head of the nation's government. He carried out his executive duties now in the midst of the bustle and clamor of hurrying messengers and clattering typewriters. Except for the typewriters, it was like one of the old one-night camps of George Washington during the Revolutionary War.

UPSTAIRS IN the same building were the offices of the War and Navy departments, the Commissary and Ordnance departments. From here pulsed the orders which encouraged to resistance the rest of the country. The ragged lines that retreated with stubborn slowness before the vicious Green Gas had their backs to the Mississippi now. The way was still open for orders from Jacksonville, through Alabama, Mississippi, Louisiana and Texas.

But the President had foreseen that the government might be bottled up in Florida if it were pushed further south. So there was a fleet of ships waiting at Tampa to carry the executives and refugees across the Gulf of Mexico to Galveston. Congress had adjourned voluntarily, leaving plenary powers in the hands of the President. If anything should happen to the Chief Executive, the threads of defense would be snapped. Therefore, the Presidential offices were very temporary in nature.

It was in this courtroom, a far cry from the White House fireside, that the President, with Z-7 at his side, received the man who had brought in the captured gunboat.

And it was Z-7 who uttered a hoarse gasp when he saw the

face of that man, as he entered through the broad doors at the far end of the room. Z-7 took a quick, glad step forward, then checked himself, checked the expression of joyous welcome on his lips. He glanced sideways at the President, who was also looking at Jimmy Christopher, but without recognition. The President had met Operator 5 several times, but always under circumstances of grave stress. Several of his predecessors had had occasion to become very intimate with Operator 5. But this incumbent of the executive chair had never had the opportunity to learn to know him well. Thus, he did not know that the man who stood before him now was the man whom he thought dead, and whose name he had, himself, officially struck from the rolls of the Intelligence Service.

Jimmy Christopher met the gaze of Z-7, and he shook his head slightly. Z-7 gulped, and said nothing.

The President spoke graciously: "Whoever you are, young man, you are welcome. You have done a very brave thing, you and your followers, and you have helped to save several hundred people from the Green Gas. If we should ever drive the invader from our country, I shall see to it that your deed is properly recognized. In the meantime, is there anything I can offer you in the way of reward? If it is within my power, I shall be glad to do it for you."

Jimmy stepped forward eagerly, while Z-7 watched him, biting his lip.

"I don't want any reward, sir. But I'd like a chance to do something more for my country. I'd like a chance to get in behind the enemy lines. I want to try to discover the secret of the Green Gas."

The President started. "You—think you could do that?"

"I don't know, sir. But it's worth a try. I was working along those lines in New York, when I was forced to—capture that ship, and escape. I want to get back."

"How do you propose to do that?"

JIMMY INDICATED his uniform, that of a Central Empire Naval Commander, which he had taken from the commander of the gunboat. "Once inside the enemy lines, this will pass me along. I'll want a plane, and a pilot to drop me somewhere in the occupied territory."

The President hesitated. "Your chances would be slim. If you were caught in that uniform, the best you could hope for would be the firing squad—or the executioner's block."

Jimmy shrugged. "What of it? It's better than sniffing the Green Gas."

The President glanced inquiringly at Z-7, who nodded.

"All right, young man. I think it can be arranged. When would you like to have this plane?"

"Right now, sir. Every hour that we delay means more territory flooded with gas. I'd like to leave at once."

"But—!"

"Excuse me, sir," Z-7 broke in. "There's a plane being warmed up at the field at Eastport right now. Lieutenant Dinsmore was to leave in a few minutes to deliver orders to the Army of the West. I think it would be wise to let this young man have that plane."

127

"If you say so," the President conceded. He motioned to one of his secretaries, directed: "Make out an order to Major King at the airport, to place at the disposal of the bearer the plane that is being prepared for Lieutenant Dinsmore."

He explained to Jimmy: "We are reduced to sending written notes and verbal messages. The great power plants of the East are in the hands of the enemy, and our telephone service is at a standstill."

While the secretary was typing the order, and while the President was signing it, Jimmy cast a grateful glance at Z-7. He realized that Z-7 was risking his position as the head of the Intelligence by keeping secret the fact that this was Operator 5 who was being given a plane and the facilities for returning to the enemy lines.

The President himself handed Jimmy the written order, and suddenly laughed, said: "By Jove! I've neglected to ask your name. You must pardon me, young man, but there are so many things on my mind these days. What *is* your name?"

Jimmy hesitated. "I—"

He stopped as an interruption came from the door. The harsh voice of General Redfern, tinged slightly with excitement:

"Pardon the intrusion, Mr. President. This is of the utmost importance. My men have just sent back a prisoner who was caught crossing over from the enemy lines in civilian clothes. Here he is!"

Two of Redfern's men brought in between them a sweating, bald-headed man. Jimmy Christopher recognized him at once, and did not need the general's next words to identify the man.

The general announced triumphantly: "This man is the Baron zu Lambrecht, Marshal of the Central Empire. He has come across the lines as a spy, and must be shot!"

Oscar, Baron zu Lambrecht, squirmed, exclaimed: "No, no! I am not a spy. I flee from the wrath of the new Emperor!"

Redfern laughed. "That's a good story!"

Jimmy had stepped back several paces, trying to keep in the shadow. The appearance of General Redfern was the last thing in the world he could have wanted at that moment. Of the few men who knew him by sight as Operator 5, Redfern was one. Jimmy had his order for the plane. He had said good-by to Diane and Nan and the others on the gunboat. If he could get out of here without being noticed....

REDFERN HAD stepped up to the President's desk. "Mr. President, this man must be shot. To spare him would kill the morale of the entire Defense Force. They know how their friends and relatives have suffered; they've seen brothers and sisters and mothers and fathers bloated and blue in death from the effects of the Green Gas. If you show you are soft, and spare this man, who was virtually the second in command of the Central Empire, what do you think our boys will say?"

The President nodded. "I see no reason for clemency. This man was found inside our lines in civilian clothes. That makes him out a spy by all the rules of warfare. I order him to be shot!"

Oscar zu Lambrecht, who spoke English fairly well, grew white. His eyes searched the room for some means of escape. And as he looked around, General Redfern looked around, too, and spotted Jimmy Christopher's Central Empire uniform.

129

Oscar zu Lambrecht burst out in a torrent of words in his native tongue, thinking that here was a compatriot of his. But Redfern glimpsed Jimmy's face, and suddenly roared:

"That man is Operator 5!"

Immediately a hush descended upon the room. The clattering of typewriters ceased. The President stared with unbelief, and Z-7 stirred uncomfortably. Redfern swung on the Chief Executive. Baron Oscar zu Lambrecht was forgotten in his vindictive excitement. "Mr. President, I thought Operator 5 had been killed in that mad assassination of the Emperor Maximilian. I was almost willing to forgive him for having brought the scourge of the Green Gas upon us, because I thought that he had sacrificed his own life. But he wasn't so self-sacrificing." The fiery general's lips curled in scorn. "He must have been damned sure that he would escape alive. And he did. What's he doing in the uniform of the Central Empire?"

The President turned, frowning, on Z-7. "Is it true, Z-7?" he asked. "Is this man Operator 5? And did you stand by and advise me to give him a plane?"

Z-7 lowered his eyes before the accusing glance of the President. Before he could reply, Jimmy Christopher stepped forward, pushing Oscar zu Lambrecht aside. "It's true, sir," he said quietly. "I am Operator 5. But I didn't kill Maximilian. Another man did it in my place. But even if I had done it, I don't see why I am hated so much—"

General Redfern exploded. "He doesn't see why he's hated so much—the man whose deed caused the death of more than a million innocent Americans. You were supposed to give yourself up, Operator 5, to prevent the release of the Green Gas. Instead of that, you resorted to cheap assassination to save your own life, not caring what the consequences would be. *You are going to be court-martialed, Mr. Operator 5!*"

"I tell you," Jimmy reiterated, "I didn't kill Maximilian—"

"That's what *you* say. We'll see what a military judge thinks about it. Mr. President, I demand the right to arrest this man!"

The President nodded reluctantly. "I'm afraid I must grant General Redfern's request. At your trial, if the evidence should show—"

"But, Mr. President, what of my trip behind the enemy lines? Let me try to discover the secret of the Green Gas—"

"I'm sorry, Operator 5. As the matter stands now, until it is proved to the contrary, you are not the type of person to be entrusted with such a mission."

Redfern growled to the guards who had brought Oscar in: "Place him under arrest. If he resists, shoot—"

Jimmy Christopher had been watching Z-7 edge toward the wall, near the electric light switch. His body was tense, taut, as he saw Z-7's hand reach up, press the button. The room was plunged into darkness. In the flickering instant before the lights went out, a look of deep understanding passed between those two men: Z-7, the Chief of the United States Intelligence, and Operator 5, the agent in whom Z-7 had more confidence than in any other man under him.

JIMMY KNEW what Z-7 was doing. He was risking his whole career by that simple act of pressing the light button.

But he was doing it because he firmly believed that Operator 5 was more valuable to the United States at large than in a military prison, awaiting court-martial.

In the sudden darkness, pandemonium broke loose. Redfern's apoplectic voice sounded above the excited shouts and cries of the typists and secretaries. A rifle exploded in the hands of one of the soldiers. Redfern leaped through the air at the spot where Jimmy Christopher had stood. But Jimmy was no longer there. Acting with the speed and coördination of well-trained muscles and mind, Operator 5 had ducked to one side, run along the wall down the end aisle beside the row of typewriter desks. He reached the door before the uncertain light from several flashlights caught him. Redfern shrieked: "There he goes! Shoot to kill!" Orange flame spurted behind him, slugs crashed into the wall.

Redfern shouted, above the din of the rifle and revolver explosions: "Cover the door! Don't let him leave!"

More lead whined past Jimmy, and he saw in the split second before he reached the door that two soldiers, obeying Redfern's command, had slid around and were standing before the doorway, with rifles set to fire at him.

Thinking with the speed of lightning, Jimmy Christopher pulled up short, dropped to his knees beside a typewriter desk just as the soldiers fired. Their slugs whined over his head, smashing the glass of a window. Before they could shoot again, Jimmy pushed the man at the desk off his chair with a single, desperate shove, and raised the chair, hurled it at the two soldiers. More shots were coming from behind, but they were not so thick, for there was danger of hitting others in the room.

Jimmy seized the single moment of confusion after he had hurled the chair, and leaped squarely across the aisle, through the window whose glass had been smashed by the shots of the soldiers. Just as he went through, someone switched on the lights inside, and that helped Jimmy, for it momentarily blinded those within, made it harder to see him in the comparative darkness outside.

There were mingled cries and shouts, and above them, Redfern's infuriated voice: "Get outside. He can't get away. Shoot him on sight!"

Jimmy was on the patio that surrounded the courthouse. He raced across it, leaped to the ground, and ran fifty feet toward the square, where he saw the staff car in which General Redfern had returned. He heard running steps behind him, turned for a second and saw shapes piling out of the window behind him. Flashes of flame stabbed the night, and lead tugged at his left sleeve. He reached the squad car, and now drew his own revolver, poked it at the startled uniformed chauffeur in the driver's seat. "Get out!" he snapped.

The driver almost rolled out of the car at the desperate glint in his eye, and at the menace of his gun.

Jimmy slid in under the wheel, gunned the accelerator, and was rewarded with the deep-throated purr of the motor. It had been running!

Almost with the same motion he shifted, released the clutch, and was off, with lead pouring into the back of the car, drumming a mad tattoo on the tonneau, and shrieking through the canvas top. Jimmy zigzagged across the square, turned left into a street that led to the river. In a moment he had left his pursuit behind. He could hear the hullabaloo he had left, above the roar of his motor. He was going in the wrong direction for the airport. He should have gone northwest, in order to hit Norwood Avenue, which would take him across Moncrief Creek toward the airport; instead, he was traveling south, toward the James River. He thought quickly, for at the rate of speed he was making there wasn't much time for cogitation. He could make a right turn at the next corner, and swing around behind the courthouse; or he could turn left and head for Talleyrand Avenue, which would take him through the heart of the city. He turned right. They would never look for him to come right back to the spot he had escaped from. And he was correct.

It was as dead as a doornail behind the courthouse as he sped past—except for one figure, which he recognized. Baron Oscar zu Lambrecht!

THERE WAS no mistaking the baron's face, etched in the glare of the headlights, as the stout man attempted to hasten across the street, which he had been furtively crossing. Jimmy stepped on the brakes, skidding to a stop, and Lambrecht halted in the middle of the street, with his hands above his head. "Do not shoot!" he begged.

Jimmy leaned out of the car, and Oscar's eyes widened at sight of the uniform. "You!" he exclaimed.

Jimmy grinned. "It looks like you got away in the confusion, too, Oscar. Get in. I might as well take you along. I might find you useful."

The amazed incredulity in Lambrecht's face gave way to

relieved gratitude when he discovered that Jimmy was going to take him along. He clambered into the car, and Jimmy got going again. Not a soul had appeared to question them. Everybody was heading out toward the center of the city, in the wild manhunt that Redfern had started.

As Jimmy tooled the car along the waterfront it looked no different from numerous other army cars that were using the streets. As long as they didn't start to halt every auto, they might have a chance of getting away.

Oscar, sitting with his hands clenched in his lap, asked: "You are truly Operator 5?"

Jimmy nodded. "Why did you cross the lines, Oscar? Redfern was dizzy. You couldn't have come as a spy."

"I am not a spy," Lambrecht said sadly. "I spoke the truth when I said that I flee from the new Emperor. He hates me. But tell me—how do you hope to escape from these mad Yankees?"

Jimmy chuckled as he swung west into the old King's Road, now State Street. He had angled far enough out so that he had avoided the congested portion of State Street. "We'll head up to Eastport," he said. "There's a plane waiting there—if they don't reach the airport before we do—and I'm going to take off at once—toward the Central Empire lines. Do you want to come along, Oscar?"

Lambrecht shuddered. "I dare not! If Rudolph captured me, he would surely behead me—with his own hands!"

"And if you stay here," Jimmy told him cheerfully, "they'll surely shoot you. So take your choice."

"I—I go with you," Lambrecht said, sighing. "I am more at

home among my own people. I—perhaps I could hide there, better. Here, I am lost."

Jimmy nodded. "Okay, Oscar, I'll make a deal with you. I help you, and you help me. Right now I guess I'm a little out of favor with my own government. But that won't last. And if you can help me against Rudolph, and we stop the invasion, I think I can promise you sanctuary in America. Mind you, Oscar, I don't like you, and I have no use for you personally. But it's a working arrangement. In time of war we can't be finicky. And I think I'll be reasonably safe with you—as long as you're so deathly afraid of Rudolph. Is it a deal, Oscar?"

"It is a deal," Lambrecht said softly. But Jimmy Christopher didn't see the crafty gleam in the eyes of the Baron Oscar zu Lambrecht, former Marshal of the Central Empire....

CHAPTER 12
A DEAL IN DEATH

I T WAS two hours before dawn when the swift two-seater that Jimmy had commandeered at Jacksonville, on the strength of his written order from the President, landed at the Holmes Airport in Flushing, on the other side of the East River from Manhattan Island.

They had flown over the Carolinas, over Virginia and Maryland. And looking down, Jimmy felt sick at heart to see the waste and desolation that lay over all those flat lands. There was not a soul to be seen in motion down there. Flying very low in the night, with Baron Lambrecht in the forward cockpit, Jimmy had looked over the side constantly, and had discerned fields where bodies lay quiet, immovable in death. The moon shed a pale and morbid radiance over the stillness that was on the earth below.

The Green Gas had passed over all this territory, which had once teemed with life. And now there was no life here at all; only bloated, hideous death. There was a lump in Jimmy Christopher's throat, as his hands automatically played with the controls. His eyes stared through the goggles at the back of Oscar zu Lambrecht's fat neck, and he felt a red haze of rage. This was one of the men who had brought the bloated death to America. In that moment Jimmy hated Lambrecht as he had never hated another man. Somewhere down there, Jimmy's own father might be lying, discolored and hideous. And here sat a man in front of him….

Jimmy Christopher restained an ungoverned impulse to take his hands from the controls and to wrap them around that fat throat.

He landed in darkness, finding the Holmes Airport by instinct. He had used that field often in the past, and he knew just how many minutes it was from Flushing Bay at the rate of speed he was making. He threw out a flare before he hit ground, and he taxied to a perfect stop.

The field was deserted, forgotten. With the advent of the Central Empire invaders, many of the flying fields on the outskirts of the city had become unused. No American was permitted to fly a plane, and most of the Empire's aircraft were seaplanes. Their landing was unobserved.

Jimmy climbed out of the cockpit, helped Lambrecht out, and

they walked two miles to the recently completed Triborough Bridge, linking Manhattan, Queens and the Bronx. Before starting out on their walk, Jimmy treated Lambrecht's face, using the small, compact kit of makeup material that he always carried with him. He set up a small mirror, used a light hooked up to the plane's battery, and proceeded to darken the baron's cheeks with pigment, to thicken his eyebrows with paint, and to change the appearance of his nose by inserting two tiny, paper-thin metal plates in his nostrils that distended them.

When he was finished, he stood back and surveyed his handiwork. "You'll pass, Oscar. In the dark, with what I've done to you, you'll never be recognized!"

Lambrecht took a look in the mirror, and his fat face was wreathed in a smile for the first time that day. "You are right," he said. "I would not know myself."

"Let's go, then."

They set out across country. As they came near the approach to the Triborough Bridge, a sentry hailed them. Jimmy Christopher whispered to Lambrecht: "If you have any funny ideas, Oscar, get rid of them. You keep silent, and let me do the talking. If you talk, you'll get shot—after coming a thousand miles to escape that fate!" He tapped significantly the holstered revolver in his belt. "I trust you, Oscar, but I've got my hand on this, just in case!"

To the sentry, Jimmy used the arrogant tone of a Naval Commander of the Grand Fleet, which his uniform bespoke him. "Our car broke down two miles back. You will find your officer, and tell him to get us another car to take us to head-quarters—at once!"

IN TEN minutes they were speeding across the bridge in a staff car, behind a stiff army chauffeur. Lambrecht spoke not a word. The driver swung south after reaching Manhattan, and it was then that Jimmy tapped him on the shoulder, told him to pull up. He obeyed, and Jimmy poked his revolver in the chauffeur's back, ordered him to come around in the rear. He trussed the man up and gagged him with his own belt and his own necktie and handkerchief, and placed him on the floor. Then he motioned Lambrecht to the front seat.

A patrol passed them, and the petty officer in charge saluted respectfully, left them strictly alone. The uniforms were enough for him.

Jimmy waited till the patrol had passed out of sight. Then he said: "Now, Oscar, we can get down to business. I'll tell you why I was so good to you, and brought you back here with me. There were three men living who knew the location of the formula for the Green Gas"—he watched Lambrecht carefully out of narrowed eyes, saw him start perceptibly. "Now that Maximilian is dead, there are only two who know where the formula is. Well, there are going to be three in on the secret again. Because you're going to tell me!"

Lambrecht sat very still. Nothing moved but his lips. "You—ask me to betray my country and my Emperor?"

Jimmy laughed shortly. "What has your country and your Emperor done for you? They've made you a fugitive. You can't go back. On the other hand, I promise you safety and a pension from the United States for the help you are going to give me this night. Once your Emperor is deprived of the Green Gas, our chances of driving him from the country are increased a thousand percent—in spite of his big guns and modern equipment. To stay here means death for you. To help me may mean safety."

"You are right—" at any other time, Jimmy might have been suspicious of this easy acquiescence, but tonight he was willing to take any chance; to risk everything on a single throw—"I will tell you," Lambrecht went on. "But you must remember your promise. A safe refuge for me. If you succeed in doing this thing that you plan, your country will grant whatever you ask. You must ask complete safety and a large pension for me—enough for me to live as I would live in my own country."

"I promise."

"There will be great danger to you. And you must go alone. Those at headquarters will recognize me more quickly than these men at the bridge."

"All right." Jimmy was impatient. "Talk."

Lambrecht took a deep breath. "In your Sub-Treasury Building, there is a great vault underground, where bullion is kept. There is also a small vault where were kept rare and valuable papers of your national government."

Jimmy nodded tightly. "I know that vault."

"It is there that the formula for the Green Gas is deposited. A lieutenant and six men stand guard day and night. The vault is fireproof, safe against weather, bombs and burglars. The big vault is operated by complicated time locks and levers; but the smaller vault needs only a key, which, when inserted, makes an electrical contact. Long ago, our secret agents obtained a duplicate of that key. And when we captured New York, the Emperor chose that place for the formula. He had a key, Rudolph had one, and I—have one."

Lambrecht drew from his waistcoat pocket, with shaking fingers, a long, thin leather sheath, about five inches in length. From it he withdrew a shiny metal key. It was three times as long as the average key, and very flat. "There are five keyholes in the door of the vault," he said. "This must be inserted in the second from the left, and the door automatically slides back. Within is the formula. Everything else has been cleaned out."

JIMMY TOOK the key. He believed what Lambrecht told him, for it checked to a certain extent with what he had heard from Willfred. His eyes were gray, cold. "I've passed the building recently," he said. "It's surrounded by troops."

"That uniform should get you through. It will be at the vault that you will meet with difficulty. The lieutenant has instructions to shoot to kill anybody who enters the passage leading to the vault, except the Emperor, or myself. Doubtless now he would shoot me, too. No questions are asked. It is death to enter that corridor."

JIMMY SAID: "Well, we'll see," and started the car once more, drove downtown toward the Treasury Building. They passed absolutely no civilians on the way, and Jimmy wondered about that, until Lambrecht told him that Rudolph must have put into effect a regulation that he had often urged his father to enforce—a curfew law, requiring all Americans in the city to stay off the streets after seven o'clock.

"Rudolph," said the baron, "is a sadistic beast who glories in the sight of human pain and suffering. Your people would have been far better off if Maximilian had remained alive."

"So I've been hearing," Jimmy told him tartly.

They parked at a distance from the Treasury Building, on a side street where the ruins of tall buildings demolished by the bombardment made it impossible for traffic to pass through. Jimmy pulled the car into a corner that was free from debris, and turned off the lights. "You stay here, Oscar," he said. "If you see me come running, get the motor started for a quick getaway. If you hear a lot of shooting, and I don't come—"Jimmy shrugged—"you'll have to work out your own salvation."

He turned and walked away, striding stiffly, with the arrogance that befitted his uniform. Several patrols that he met saluted him punctiliously, even stood aside for him to pass. Before the imposing facade of the structure where the United States Government had once stored its bullion, a detail of troops was drawn up at attention. Jimmy stopped at the corner, wondering at this.

A young Central Empire officer, standing nearby, glanced at him, and Jimmy said: "Why are those troops standing at attention?"

The officer appeared surprised. "Didn't you know? The Emperor is coming here. He is due at any moment."

"The Emperor? Why?"

"He comes to get the formula for the Green Gas. All the manufactured supply was exhausted in the big push yesterday and today. For tomorrow, the Emperor needs two tons of gas. He is bringing chemists, who will copy the formula, put the original back in the vault, so that they can compound the gas. Where have you been that you do not know of this? The officers have all been apprised of what is taking place."

The man looked at him suspiciously, and Jimmy said hastily: "I have been at sea. I docked only tonight."

The other glanced at his uniform. "Oh, yes. You must be part of the northern fleet, that is stopping here en route to blockade the Gulf of Mexico."

Jimmy started. If the Gulf of Mexico were blockaded, it would mean that all communication would be cut off between the executive and the western American armies. He hid his consternation, nodded casually. "This is interesting, about the formula. These poor chemists do not know that the completion of their task means their death, eh?"

The officer laughed. "Everybody knows it but they. They have been kept alone all this time—two hundred of them, as you probably know. Each week, five more are used to make the gas. In twenty weeks they will have to find more chemists."

JIMMY'S MIND was working swiftly. He excused himself to the officer, made his way closer to the entrance of the Treasury Building. An officer in charge of the troops saluted him, and Jimmy said:

"I am from the fleet. I have received orders to meet His Imperial Majesty in the Treasury Building, for special instructions. He has not arrived yet?"

The officer said: "No, sir. But he is expected in a few moments."

Jimmy nodded. "I'll wait for him inside. Those were my instructions."

He passed through the cordon of troops, walked up the broad steps, and entered the gloomy interior of the building. His presence here was taken for granted. There were dozens of other officers about, and it was evidently proper for them all to be here. No doubt the opening of the vault was an occasion of sorts.

Jimmy moved down the corridor leading to the staircase at the rear, which he knew from previous visits led down to the vaults. Four or five officers were standing in a group outside a room off the corridor, the door of which was open. They were laughing and joking among themselves and looking into this room. At the doorway, two uniformed soldiers stood on guard with bayoneted rifles.

Jimmy peered inside, and saw a group of five pale young men in civilian clothes chatting among themselves. They were pale, anemic-looking, studious young men.

Jimmy joined the group of officers in the corridor, and one of them offered him a cigarette. "We were just watching the lambs, being prepared for the sacrifice. We were wondering how they would feel if they knew that they were to be dead by this time tomorrow!"

Jimmy shrugged. "What is death? We may all meet it tomorrow."

The officer laughed. "There is little chance. While we have the Green Gas, this war is a holiday. We have had no casualties to speak of in three weeks."

Jimmy said: "This is the first time I have seen these lambs. I have been at sea so much."

"You have missed good entertainment. We come here whenever the formula is to be copied, and watch them."

"Do they all go down to copy it?"

"No. Only two. The formula, it is said, is kept on a sheet of foolscap which has been cut in half. Each of the two copies one half. Then all five of them are taken up to the laboratories."

"I see," said Jimmy. He bowed to the officers, and moved down the corridor. He was familiar with the layout of the Treasury Building. It had, on one occasion, been his day to take charge of the special guards placed here by the Intelligence Department in order to frustrate the raid of the sabotage agents of a foreign power. Jimmy Christopher had covered every inch of the place in making the arrangements, which had resulted in the failure of the raid and the capture of the foreign agents. Jimmy recalled, with the vividness of a camera recording, that the room those five youths were in had formerly been the office of the special agents of the Treasury Department assigned to the building. He recalled, also, that the room next to it connected by an adjoining door, and that it was possible to reach that room through a door around the bend in the corridor, just past the staircase.

He rounded the corridor, and stood beside that door while several men walked past. He waited for a moment when he was not observed, and quickly passed into the room. There was no light here, and he crossed quickly, carefully turned the knob leading to the room in which the five chemists sat. He opened

The door closed, shutting the Purple Emperor inside!

the door a crack, peered through. He could see the open corridor door, could see the group of officers that he had just left. And he could hear the low murmur of conversation from the five chemists. He pushed the door open a bit further, so that he could get a view of them. The two guards in the corridor were invisible, because they stood on either side of the doorway. Suddenly, the officers outside tensed, as someone near the entrance called out: "The Emperor comes!"

IN A moment there came the tread of many feet, and Emperor Rudolph I appeared in the doorway, accompanied by a dozen gorgeously attired officers. The Emperor looked into the room, and Jimmy narrowed the crack of his door. It was the first glimpse he had had of Rudolph, and he restrained an impulse to shoot the man down. He knew at that moment just how Plugger Dugan must have felt. But to kill Rudolph would do no more good than the killing of Maximilian had accomplished. The Green Gas would still be a menace. Through the crack, Jimmy heard Rudolph say: "So you are the chemists? Two of you, come with us!"

He ventured to open the door a little more, saw that the officers with Rudolph had crowded into the room, and that two of the young chemists had stepped forward. Rudolph turned to go, and the officers followed. Jimmy pushed open the door, strode boldly into the room, and made himself a part of the Emperor's entourage. He followed the group down the staircase, along the corridor that led to the small vault.

A lieutenant and a detail of men were on guard at the door,

just as Oscar had said. The Emperor ordered gruffly: "You may retire, Lieutenant!"

The detail and the officer filed through the Emperor's escort, and passed out of the corridor. The two chemists and the officers, with Jimmy among them, crowded close. One man in a field marshal's uniform, at the Emperor's elbow, said:

"The secret of the gas is well guarded indeed, sire."

Rudolph nodded. "Marshal Kremer, you may have the honor of opening the vault." He handed the field marshal a long key which was an exact duplicate of the one that Jimmy had in his pocket.

Marshal Kremer said: "Thank you, sire," and inserted the key in the second of five keyholes in the wall of the vault. There was a *click,* and a door alongside the row of keyholes began to slide away. A moment before, no one would have suspected that there was a door there. When it was open, Kremer left the key in the keyhole and Rudolph stepped inside the yawning vault, clicked on the electric lights within. He busied himself inside for a few moments, then came out holding a sheet of foolscap.

"This is the first half," he announced. "You—"indicating one of the two chemists—"sit down and copy it." He pointed to a small desk along the wall of the corridor, which had once been the desk of the vault attendant.

The chemist bowed, took the foolscap reverently and seated himself, drew from his pocket pencil and paper.

Rudolph said: "I will bring out the other half," and stepped into the vault. The moment he was inside, Jimmy pushed past Marshal Kremer, and pulled the key from the slot. He had moved so swiftly that no one present realized what had happened until the huge vault door began to slide closed. There was a startled cry from within, and they saw the figure of Rudolph leaping from a corner of the vault. But he was too late. The door slid to with a slam of finality, shutting the Emperor of the Central Empire inside.

Kremer was the first to understand what had taken place. He swung on Jimmy Christopher, his hand going to his holster, but Jimmy smilingly held out to him the twisted, broken end of the key. He had inserted it in another of the five keyholes, and had broken off the protruding end.

Kremer paled. "The Emperor!" he exclaimed. "He will suffocate!"

"That is true," Jimmy said. "Unless I release him."

The officers closed in on Jimmy, grimly, purposefully. Jimmy surveyed them coolly, not raising a hand to defend himself. He merely said to Kremer: "Tell these fools to restrain themselves. I am the only one who can get your Emperor out of that vault before he suffocates."

The officers checked themselves at that statement, and Kremer demanded: "Who are you?"

"Never mind. If you want your Emperor alive, you must meet my terms. Speak quickly. A man cannot live long in a sealed vault."

"What do you mean? What are your terms?"

"That sheet with half the formula—" Jimmy jerked his head toward the foolscap—"you will destroy it."

Kremer shouted: "No! You are mad!"

Jimmy shrugged. "That is too bad."

"Search him," Kremer ordered frantically. "He must have a key!"

JIMMY ALLOWED the rough hands of the officers to pull off his tunic, to search every inch of his clothing and his body. The operation took ten minutes, and they found nothing.

Jimmy said politely: "And now that you have had your fun, gentlemen, suppose you make up your minds. Will you have your Emperor, or your formula?"

Kremer looked at him wildly. "How do we know that you can open the vault? You have no key."

"You must take my word for it."

"Your word? Who are you?"

"I am Operator 5," Jimmy announced simply.

Marshal Kremer was a gray-haired, military-looking man. His features were sharp, clear-cut. Now he wore an expression of utter incredulity. "That cannot be. Operator 5 is dead."

Jimmy shook his head. "The man who killed Maximilian was not Operator 5. My identification is right there—" he nodded toward his personal belongings, which had been strewn on the desk alongside the parchment containing half of the formula. "I see you opened that silver case, but you didn't read the credentials in it. Why don't you?"

Marshal Kremer picked up the flat silver case, read the card therein, protected by a sheet of cellophane. It was as follows:

THE WHITE HOUSE
Washington

To Whom It May Concern:

The identity of the bearer of this letter must be kept strictly confidential.

He is Operator 5 of the United States Intelligence Service.

The signature below it was the familiar one of the President of the United States.

While Kremer was reading it, Jimmy glanced about him, reflected that it probably had more weight now, among the enemy, than it would have among his own people.

Kremer looked up from the paper. Indecision showed in his eyes.

Jimmy urged: "If you destroy that formula, and if I fail to open the door, you will still have me here; I will be in your power. On the other hand, I give you the word of Operator 5 that I can and will open that vault."

For a moment, Kremer hesitated. He glanced questioningly at the other officers, seemed to find confirmation in their gaze. He nodded jerkily, his clear eyes meeting Jimmy's. "I will do it! A man as brave as you cannot be a liar. With this sheet destroyed, the formula will be gone forever. We shall no longer have the Green Gas. But the Emperor must be rescued from death in the vault."

The Marshal seized the parchment from the stupefied chemist, tore it through, once, twice. "There! Now do your part. Quick, man!"

"Pardon me," said Jimmy. He took the pieces of the parchment from Kremer's hand, picked up a book of matches, lit one and applied it. The parchment burned to ashes. He crumpled the ashes, blew them into the air.

"Now!" He stepped close to the chemist, put a hand into that young man's coat pocket, and, under the startled eyes of all the officers, he produced the key which he had brought in with him.

"Seize him!" Marshal Kremer roared. "What a prize for the Emperor!"

But Jimmy Christopher had not been napping. He had anticipated the command, and he had prepared for it. The instant he drew the key from the chemist's pocket with his left hand, his right darted to the holster of another Central Empire officer standing nearby. It came away with a heavy, deadly automatic. And in that same heartbeat of time, Operator 5 had lunged toward the door, nimbly avoiding the hands grasping for him.

For a scant moment he poised there in the entrance to the vault, automatic fisted, holding the Purple Emperor's bloodhounds at bay. "This is just the beginning!" he shouted. "See how you like fighting Americans without the Green Gas!"

And with that, as an enraged clamor burst from the men in the vault room, Operator 5 sprinted up the stairway, vanished....

A GRIM group of men were seated about a table in the temporary headquarters of the President of the United States, in Jacksonville, Florida. In the center of the table sat the President himself. At his right was Brigadier-General Redfern. At his left was General Lukas. Across the table from them, alone, sat Z-7, chief of the American Intelligence. Deep shadows circled his eyes. His mouth was drawn into a straight, pained line. Now and then he glanced at the windows, where dawn was beginning

153

to shade the sky with gray. And then he settled wearily in the chair again, listening to the others.

The President was speaking: "It's hard to believe. But the evidence is unassailable, and the conclusion of this court martial is just. Z-7, we find you guilty of concealing Operator 5's identity, of furthering his traitorous plans, and of aiding him materially to make good his escape.

"At any other time, because of your long record of faithful service, we might be inclined to be lenient with you. But the nation is now at war. Your acts amount to treason. There can be but one verdict—one sentence."

Z-7's black eyes took on a hard, cold light. He gripped the arms of his chair with white-knuckled hands, rose slowly from the seat, stood erect and proud. The President took a sheet of paper which General Redfern had prepared, affixed his signature to it, read it in a grave, strained voice: "It is therefore the judgment of this court-martial that Z-7, formerly chief of the United States Intelligence Service, be removed from his post of honor, and that he be executed as a traitor before a firing squad." The Chief Executive paused, glanced up at Z-7 with sorrow in his eyes. "It's nearly dawn. The execution will take place then. Has the prisoner anything to say?"

Z-7 raised his chin, cleared his throat. "Yes! I would do it again. I shall never regret that I staked my life on Operator 5!"

As he finished speaking, sounds of a sudden commotion came from the stairway leading to the President's quarters. A sentinel who had been stationed outside the door burst inside. "Sorry! There's a lot of people outside, saying they have to see you."

The Chief Executive rose, leaned his hands on the heavy table. "Who are they?"

"One of 'em's Operator 5!"

"Let them come in!"

The doors swung wide, and Operator 5, still wearing the uniform of a Central Empire Naval Commander, smeared with grease from his headlong flight from New York, entered the room. Behind him came Diane Elliot, Nan, Timmy, Slips, and a host of others. Cheers rose from them as they marched toward the scene of Z-7's court-martial.

They came to a stop. The President asked: "What can I do for you?"

Operator 5 laid his hand on Z-7's shoulder, gripped it. "I've come to take my medicine, Mr. President. I wouldn't want another man—Z-7—to pay the piper for me. But I also want to tell you the good news. There will be no more Green Gas. I destroyed the formula myself last night in New York."

"And I want to tell you something, too, Mr. President," Slips McGuire blurted. "Operator 5 never killed Maximilian. That thick-skulled Plugger Dugan done that." He waved his hand, indicating all the refugees from Norfolk. "I've made these folks see the light. How about you?"

For the first time in three weeks, the President of the United States smiled.

"I don't know you from Adam," he replied, "but I *do* believe you!" He glanced at Redfern and Lukas, and, as both of them nodded, went on: "As Commander-in-Chief of the Federal Forces, I now appoint Jimmy Christopher as the generalissimo in charge of all maneuvers against the ruthless enemies who strive to crush our nation. And I also negate the sentence imposed on Z-7."

There was a reverent hush in the room. These people knew that history was in the making. A sound like a sigh rose from them.

Operator 5 shook Z-7 by the hand, heartily, and said: "Thank you, Mr. President. I shall do my best. And I am sure that with the rebirth of the American fighting spirit, the courage of the frontiersmen and plainsmen and early settlers who carved this country from the wilderness—we will drive the Purple Emperor's invaders into the sea. We have just begun to fight!"

POPULAR HERO PULPS AVAILABLE NOW:

THE SECRET 6
- ❑ #1: The Red Shadow — $13.95
- ❑ #2: House of Walking Corpses — $13.95
- ❑ #3: The Monster Murders — $13.95
- ❑ #4: The Golden Alligator — $13.95

OPERATOR 5
- ❑ #1: The Masked Invasion — $13.95
- ❑ #2: The Invisible Empire — $13.95
- ❑ #3: The Yellow Scourge — $13.95
- ❑ #4: The Melting Death — $13.95
- ❑ #5: Cavern of the Damned — $13.95
- ❑ #6: Master of Broken Men — $13.95
- ❑ #7: Invasion of the Dark Legions — $13.95
- ❑ #8: The Green Death Mists — $13.95
- ❑ #9: Legions of Starvation — $13.95
- ❑ #10: The Red Invader — $13.95
- ❑ #11: The League of War-Monsters — $13.95
- ❑ #12: The Army of the Dead — $13.95
- ❑ #13: March of the Flame Marauders — $13.95
- ❑ #14: Blood Reign of the Dictator — $13.95
- ❑ #15: Invasion of the Yellow Warlords — $13.95
- ❑ #16: Legions of the Death Master — $13.95
- ❑ #17: Hosts of the Flaming Death — $13.95
- ❑ #18: Invasion of the Crimson Death Cult — $13.95
- ❑ #19: Attack of the Blizzard Men — $13.95
- ❑ #20: Scourge of the Invisible Death — $13.95
- ❑ #21: Raiders of the Red Death — $13.95
- ❑ #22: War-Dogs of the Green Destroyer — $13.95
- ❑ #23: Rockets From Hell — $13.95
- ❑ #24: War-Masters from the Orient — $13.95
- ❑ #25: Crime's Reign of Terror — $13.95
- ❑ *NEW:* #26: Death's Ragged Army — $13.95

DUSTY AYRES AND HIS BATTLE BIRDS
- ❑ #1: Black Lightning! — $13.95
- ❑ #2: Crimson Doom — $13.95
- ❑ #3: The Purple Tornado — $13.95
- ❑ #4: The Screaming Eye — $13.95
- ❑ #5: The Green Thunderbolt — $13.95
- ❑ #6: The Red Destroyer — $13.95
- ❑ #7: The White Death — $13.95
- ❑ #8: The Black Avenger — $13.95
- ❑ #9: The Silver Typhoon — $13.95
- ❑ #10: The Troposphere F-S — $13.95
- ❑ #11: The Blue Cyclone — $13.95
- ❑ #12: The Tesla Raiders — $13.95

MAVERICKS
- ❑ #1: Five Against the Law — $12.95
- ❑ #2: Mesquite Manhunters — $12.95
- ❑ #3: Bait for the Lobo Pack — $12.95
- ❑ #4: Doc Grimson's Outlaw Posse — $12.95
- ❑ #5: Charlie Parr's Gunsmoke Cure — $12.95

THE MYSTERIOUS WU FANG
- ❑ #1: The Case of the Six Coffins — $12.95
- ❑ #2: The Case of the Scarlet Feather — $12.95
- ❑ #3: The Case of the Yellow Mask — $12.95
- ❑ #4: The Case of the Suicide Tomb — $12.95
- ❑ #5: The Case of the Green Death — $12.95
- ❑ #6: The Case of the Black Lotus — $12.95
- ❑ #7: The Case of the Hidden Scourge — $12.95